FLASHES IN TIME

A SHORT STORY COLLECTION

MIKKO RAUHALA

Cover design copyright © 2025 by Design by Definition
daniellefine.com

Published by Water Dragon Publishing
waterdragonpublishing.com

ISBN 978-1-964952-73-4 (Trade Paperback)

FIRST EDITION

10 9 8 7 6 5 4 3 2 1

CONTENTS

FLASHES OF SCIENCE NEAR

THE SCIENCE FAIR GOD

IN HINDSIGHT, THE TICKLING in Roger's disappearing toes should've been his first clue that hacking the nature of reality was a bad idea. But what was a young man with needs to do to impress the ladies? Larry, for one, had his gene-spliced chess master orcas, and while the school's bioethics council was frowning on the use of Kasparov DNA, the grand master's estate had shrugged and said that good old Garry would've loved bringing chess to marine life. With their blessing, and with nobody being able to prove that there had been any specific sort of foul play involved in how Larry had gotten his hands on the nucleotides, he was off to the races in the school science fair.

And Jack had gone and gotten in touch with a bunch of bona fide extra-terrestrials through his tachyon ansible. Not that the ETs were very helpful in providing humanity with scientific breakthroughs, technologies, or whatnot, but they cracked a mean pun—or at least that was Jack's working theory as to what was going on behind the universal translator at their end, what with the aliens always seeming to be quite amused with themselves without any clear reason why. Jack's machine learning algorithm was still working on reverse-engineering the original ET language under the assumption that every communique was riddled with homophones.

So really, it wasn't as if Roger had any choice but to try and become a god. In the modern competitive high school environment, anything less wasn't going to secure him a prom date with Sally Meadows, the most beautifully deadpan know-it-all in Roger's class. Sally herself would be demonstrating solutions to NP-complete problems in polynomial time using a time-looped computer. That kind of girl had standards.

It had all started so innocently, with Roger sneaking into the school's supercollider control room after hours. Desperate to make a groundbreaking discovery or two on the last night before the fair, he pushed the collider up to eleven, structural integrity be damned. It turned out the engineers had built a solid product with safety margins up the wazoo. It was the structural integrity of space-time itself that gave way first, revealing a tear into the inner workings of the Universe.

Roger, still unaware of what he'd found, reached into the collision chamber to poke at the glimmering sphere with his pen, as one does when there's uncertainty over whether touching something is likelier to bestow supernatural powers or to kill. The tear budged backward a bit, but also disintegrated whatever part of the pen Roger touched it with. He settled on the latter preliminary hypothesis.

As the metal parts of the pen seemed to disappear slightly slower than the plastic, Roger grabbed a titanium shell from a nearby shelf, where they were kept for just this sort of thing. Lo and behold, the heavy metal held the tear well enough to carry, at least for a while. Roger put the rest of the titanium shells into his backpack and mozied on into the science fair area. He was careful to drag the tear behind him to avoid accidentally running into it when the titanium gave way, which it did, twice.

The rest of the night he spent making measurements and bombarding the tear with radiation, his smile slowly widening to the extent that Garry and Sergey, the orcas in the next stall over, saw in him a kindred spirit.

•   •   •

The morning saw a tired but excited Roger slouching at his stall as the rest of the students barged in with their hypno-rays, domesticated coronaviruses, and model volcanoes, real ones being banned due to an unfortunate incident the year before. By now Roger had an inkling as to what he'd found, so he returned Jack's grin in kind as he was coming to check on his ansible.

"Happy, are we?" Jack asked. "You think you've found something to beat first contact or is it sleep deprivation?"

"That's not an 'or' question," Roger said, beaming at Jack. "Stand still for a moment, would you?" Then he gazed into his computer screen and typed in a few coordinates.

"Oh-kay," Jack said. "But I'd better not get any surprises about my fertility afterwards." He glanced at his school badge which doubled as a personal radiation detector.

"Nah. There's no particle flow toward you involved at all. Nevertheless, I shall divine that in your inside jacket pocket, you have a smartphone, a ballpoint pen running on fumes—"

Jack's snicker interrupted Roger. "That's where I keep 'em. I'm sure you've seen me take those out lots of times."

"—a couple of tiny pieces of blotter paper in a ziplock, for inspiration I'm sure, and a prophylactic best before last December, which I should hope I haven't seen you take out before, let alone many times." Roger batted his eyelashes at Jack, whose grin quickly faded.

"When'd you look into … No, you couldn't know I only had two left. What the hell's going on here?"

Roger's open hand pointed at the shiny tear in reality embedded inside his instrumentation. "I can read the Matrix, that's what the hell. But not only that. Check this. Copy-paste. You're welcome," he said with a wink.

Suddenly, Jack's jacket seemed heavier. He carefully opened up his pocket and peered in. His eyes went wide with shock.

"Dude, not cool! Felony amounts!" Jack hissed.

"Oh, right." Roger hit a few buttons and the bag deflated back into its original form.

Jack frowned. "Still. Pretty good. Pret-ty good." He glanced at his ansible, and then looked sheepishly at the floor. "I think I might as well concede, given that my contacts haven't yielded as many secrets of the Universe as I'd initially hoped."

"I'm sure you have a shot at second place, though Sally will give you a run for your money. I mean, no offense to the orcas, I've watched them play while running my experiments, and they're really good." Garry, the larger of the two, sprayed a pillar of water up into the air and waved his fin at the boys in acknowledgment, while Roger started to rise up from his chair to pat Jack on the back. "It's just a question of impaaaaact!"

Roger was splashed by some of the water flying through the air, but that wasn't why he yelped. Rather, it was at this time he wished he'd paid more attention to his feet, or the half that was left of them. He fell back on his chair and quickly heaved his left leg on the table. A shiny distortion, not unlike the tear itself, had eaten through the ball of his foot, shoe and all. A quick peek below verified that the problem was symmetric.

"What the hell?" Jack offered.

"I don't know," Roger said, frantically typing on the console. "There's some sort of repeating interference pattern in the feedback. I didn't think much of it before, but it's changed now. I wonder if it means something."

The orcas perked up, pausing their game to sing in their tank.

"You're getting unknown feedback from the Matrix and you just decided to ignore it?" Jack asked, wrinkling his nose.

"I was in a hurry to come up with something! My anti-gravity sled—"

"Didn't get off the ground?" Jack interrupted.

"—is orbiting Jupiter with a depleted battery. Turns out gravity is *really important* for keeping things where they're supposed to be."

Meanwhile, the orcas broke away from their pow wow. Garry gave Sergey some room to maneuver while the latter took the white queen and balanced it on his snout. Then he tossed the oversized chess piece toward Jack's ansible.

As soon as the piece hit the transmit button, Garry let out a loud, long wail. The room went quiet, everyone turning to look at the whale. As the whale was still just a whale, there was a collective shrug and people turned back to whatever it was they were doing.

The ansible cracked. A voice clearly patterned after Jack's but slightly higher in pitch carefully intoned: "Um, so, your moaning friend said that after careful analysis, the best 'move' seemed to be to inform us that you have a reality dysfunction on your hands. Is that right? If so, that's big." The snicker accompanying the message sounded unusually worried.

At this time, Jack's alien linguistics analyzer decided to chime in, in its pleasant female elevator voice: "93% confidence that 'reality dysfunction' also sounds like 'ersatz male genitalia' in the alien language."

"I've got to check that," Jack said and hit transmit. "Correct, we're facing a small instance of ersatz male genitalia, but we fear it's getting bigger as we speak, eating into my friend's feet. Can you advise?"

"Acknowledged." An almost completely suppressed chuckle underlined how grave the situation was. "Your friend mentioned a repeating message from the rift and thought our universal translator might help make sense of it. Please pipe it through," the alien voice continued.

"Yes! It works!" Jack rejoiced.

"91% confidence that 'pipe it through' also—" the analyzer started, but Roger reached in from his booth and slammed it shut. "Mind if I try to fix this without having to listen to ET double entendre analyses?" he said through clenched teeth.

"Sheesh, go on and rain on my parade while I'm helping. Fine, have it your way," Jack said, while preparing his device for input from Roger's setup.

That's when Larry made it to the scene. "Sorry about the chess piece. Don't know what came over Sergey. What's going on here?"

"No worries. I owe Garry and Sergey a big thank you if they managed to get the aliens to make themselves useful for a change," Jack said with a nod.

"Hell yeah!" Roger yelped. "I keep trying to paste my feet back but it's not working!"

Larry raised a finger and opened his mouth, but hesitated in formulating a sentence.

"Pipe the message through here," Jack said and offered Roger a cable.

"Here's hoping that your dad joke device can save the day after all," Roger grumbled while plugging the cable in.

"Hi guys, what's the ruckus?" Sally asked from behind Larry, who was still struggling to catch up.

"S-Sally!" Roger stuttered, his face red. "I—"

"Right, listen up, so I'll have to explain this only once," Jack cut in and pressed transmit. "To sum up, my friend Roger here has come across a tear in spacetime through which he can monitor and manipulate reality, at least at close range. However, now he's disappearing into an ersatz"—Jack paused for just a tiny moment to glance at Sally—"a reality dysfunction feet first and can't make it stop. What follows is a message of sorts that's repeating from the tear. Please respond if you can make any sense of it."

"Okay," said Sally and gave Roger an uncharacteristically quizzical eyebrow. "Wow. A reality dysfunction. That's big."

"That's what they said," Jack retorted, pointing at the ansible.

"Shut it, jackass. This is serious," Roger barked and raised his left leg on the table again. "Look, it's up to my ankles!" Indeed, the shiny distortion had eaten its way up to Roger's Achilles tendon.

"Does that hurt? The leg seems otherwise normal, which is weird for a spontaneous amputation," Larry put in.

"Tickles a bit in my imaginary toes, but I don't need an anatomy lesson, I need my feet back so that I can—" Roger glanced at Sally and stopped in his tracks. If this wasn't reversible, it'd shut down his prom dreams quicker than an embarrassing failure to top first contact.

Sally looked like she was about to say something, but right then the ansible crackled back to life. "The communique from the rift is a cryptographic challenge packet, requesting authorization for meddling with reality. I, uh, suggest that you come up with a proper response. We're not sure how much of the Universe it is going to end up sanitizing if it doesn't get what it wants. Our analysis of the data format follows," the ET said with scarcely a snicker. A diagram appeared on the ansible screen.

Jack glanced at the muted linguistics analyzer and snorted. "Roger that," he transmitted and turned to the others. "Now, Roger here is a goner, possibly along with the totality of existence, unless we can crack this thing in short order. Ideas?"

"No worries," said Sally and slapped her laptop onto the table. Then she plugged a homebrew circuit board into its USB port. "Gimme the cable."

Jack detached the cable from the ansible and handed it to Sally. "What've you got?"

"Simple. I'll read a message from my time memory stick and pipe it through to the anomaly via Roger's computer. If it helps, I'll write the same message back to the stick, completing the time loop. If it doesn't, I'll add one to the message's binary form and write that, sort of counterfactually iterating through the possible replies. Ready, Roger?"

Roger managed a nod. "Genius! But hurry, it's speeding up. My calves are tingling."

Sally flashed Roger a smile that would've made him faint if he wasn't already chock full of adrenaline. Then she typed furiously for five seconds and smashed enter.

Roger's face came alight and he stood up, happily hopping from one foot to another. "Wow! They're back! My feet are whole again! But ..." Roger hesitated and looked upon Sally with newfound awe, on top of any prom aspirations.

"But what?" Sally asked while giving another command to send the message back in time again.

Roger blinked. "I mean, the way you set it up, this is the only stable timeline, but only if you were truly committed to destroying any timeline you found yourself in where it didn't work. That's how it works, right, if you paradoxically send back a different message than you received?"

Sally shrugged. "And? The world was at stake. Potentially."

"But you didn't come in expecting the world to be at stake. You came in expecting science fair stakes."

A bellowing laughter erupted out of Sally Meadows' mouth, dropping the jaws of all the boys around her. It took a few seconds for her to catch herself and take a deep breath. Then she fixed her glasses and wiped a stray hair off to the side, with just a bit of a smirk left in the corner of her mouth. "True enough. But if it makes you feel better, for my demos pruning the counterfactual timelines is all automated. I just didn't have time to set up proper victory condition detection for this particular problem."

That was enough. Roger's desire for this girl, helped along by his adrenaline high, overcame his anxiety. "Want to go to the prom with me?" he blurted out.

Sally gave him a measuring look, a grin slowly manifesting on her face. "Maybe it's Ben Franklin effect, but I've had my fill of dates that ended rather than started at that laugh. Let's do it."

•   •   •

And that right there is how Roger Milholland (later Meadows), Sally Meadows, Jack Taylor, and Larry Lowe won their shared first prize in the Mayview High Science Fair for discovering that the world is a simulation and successfully avoiding its premature termination, even though, to be fair, Larry kind of stole the glory properly belonging to the orcas.

THE AIDE

THE DISHWASHER WAS FILLING UP FAST. It wouldn't have hurt Rick to lend a helping hand now and then, instead of laying on the couch. To be fair, he was glad to help if specifically asked to, but playing bossman could be exhausting in itself. Would've been nice if he showed more initiative sometimes. At least he vacuumed on occasion when it got too dusty for him. I guess he just somehow didn't notice the accumulating piles of dishes and empty wrappers, but if he got too sneezy, he'd take notice and do something about it.

The mail slot clanked in the foyer, and Rick again demonstrated his observational skills as long as the target was of interest. He abandoned his laptop on the sofa and swooped in like a hawk to check the mail. Must've been expecting something.

"Yes!" he bellowed from the door. "It finally arrived!"

"What's that then?" I asked and put some detergent in the machine.

"Honey, we talked about this. It's my new Aide."

"Oh, that." I supposed he'd mentioned it sometime, asked if I was interested, but having a voice in my ear constantly telling me what I should do or say hadn't exactly sounded appealing. I liked thinking that I was my own lord and master.

Rick had apparently gone ahead and ordered one anyway. Maybe he'd even said as much, I couldn't be sure. He had been pretty stoked about it though, and it's not like he wasn't always clamoring for the latest gadget. Not that I minded much, as long as he didn't break our budget. Wasn't as if I didn't invest in myself, though I tended to steer more into experiences. A proper massage did wonders to the quality of life, much more than fashionable electronics. Rick would say that the devices lasted longer, but to be honest, most of them tended to end up buried in the closet eventually anyway.

"Yeah. Just wait, you're gonna want one for yourself once you see what it can do. This is the best thing money can buy right now," Rick said while tearing the package open.

A couple of issues of a budgetary nature came into mind. "Wasn't it expensive though?"

"Well, they let you pay in installments. It'll pay for itself in no time anyway," he said and slipped the earpiece he'd unearthed from the package straight into his left ear. He never bothered with instructions. Well, it was called 'The Aide'. It was probably ready to show him the ropes.

"How do you figure? And installments? You didn't go for the expensive model, did you?" I was trying to keep my voice level, but if he'd spent half his pay for six months, I think I would've liked to have more of a say in it.

Rick's eyes pointed a bit to the side. The device must've been telling him something. "I thought it'd be worth it, as with the budget model the advertisers get their say in the Aide's recommendations. And you know what, this thing just said the exact same thing!"

I felt my brow ruffle. "So it's on the job already?"

Rick waited for a moment. "Yeah. It's saying that I've gotta connect it to my social media and stuff so that it can give proper advice geared just for me. But getting the premium model is good for just about anyone, it says. Now it serves only me and not a bunch of sponsors."

Hmh. "I suppose that does sound like solid advice."

"For sure! And now it's saying, um, right. It's recommending that I stop talking about what it's saying. I should just plain say what it says. Better for the flow of conversation, and less awkward pauses once you get used to it."

"Isn't that going a bit far though? Who knows what words it'll put into your mouth." I peeked into Rick's ear. The thing was pretty well camouflaged. I could catch a glimpse of it, but perhaps only because I knew what to look for.

Rick laughed. "Don't worry, I can put on the breaks at any time. And hey, if I say something stupid, now I can blame the Aide!"

Sigh. Like he needed any more excuses. "Right. But hey, what about the part about it paying for itself?"

"I have a career development discussion coming up at the end of the month. If I manage to impress the boss beforehand and ace the discussion, I'm hoping for a raise."

That'll be the day. "Good luck with that."

"And speaking of getting lucky ..." Rick said and moved in to put his hands on my hips.

I furrowed my brow. "Did that thing tell you to do that?"

Rick raised his hands in front of him and blinked innocently. "Don't ask, don't tell."

"It's got shitty timing. Make your own damn moves."

"Roger that."

• • •

Rick came home from work grinning like the seam of my backpack's zipper. His messages had been really mysterious, so that I couldn't make out if he was ashamed or just wanted to surprise me up close and personal. Must've been the latter then.

The smile was infectious, after all. "So did you get your raise then?"

"And then some! It just so happens that a department chief was heading for greener pastures."

My jaw dropped. "Don't tell me …"

"Yeah, they'd noticed my recent suggestions for boosting productivity. And then they gave me an interview. Which I aced, of course."

God damn. "Didn't they suspect anything?"

"I don't know, but hey, they don't really care as long as I do my job well. It ain't my fault if the other candidates haven't invested in their careers."

"Guess so."

Rick threw his jacket on the side table and approached me, raising his eyebrow. "You ever wanted to do it with a chief?"

I let out a good laugh at that, but he wasn't fazed one bit, just came in for an embrace.

"Well then, show me what that's like."

He had some new moves and whispers in my ear. It didn't seem that important in the moment where they may have been coming from.

•   •   •

I paid my groceries with a frown on my face. They'd run out of Extra Cola again. Been like that the whole week, one thing after another sold out. When I asked the cashier he said that people had been buying Extra Cola by the crate all morning. Somebody must've come up with a proper marketing gimmick.

But I guess that was a solid first world problem. I didn't really have anything to complain about, not having to count pennies in the store anymore. Still, Rick's salary having swept past mine irked me a bit. It was good for us both, of course, but I'd gotten used to being the main breadwinner, if by a small margin. But since the Aide had proven itself with Rick, it was maybe time for me to go get fitted at the mall's Aide outlet.

As I was walking past the reverse vending machines next to the store, some damn suit was standing by the bottle washing sink, pouring some cola down the drain. My cola. He had a whole bagful of it. God damn. I stared at him with my mouth open long enough for the dude to notice me, but he just turned his attention back to the task at hand and corked another bottle straight into the sewer.

I just had to ask. "What the hell are you doing?"

The dude seemed a bit perplexed, as if he wasn't quite sure himself. Then his eyes lit up and he went: "You shouldn't drink this much soda. It's bad for your health."

"Why'd you buy them then?"

He paused for a bit again. "Extra Cola is the best and cheapest cola drink available."

"Okay. Nothing to it then." Fuck. I took a couple of wary steps backward before turning around, glancing back a few times for good measure. He stayed put, getting rid of his stash one bottle at a time.

What the hell is one supposed to say to people like that? The Aide might've known. Or maybe it'd have been savvy enough to tell me to walk the fuck past the dude. Sometimes it can be good to hear the obvious solution from someone else.

I'd soon have that someone right in my ear. The next window along the promenade sported a poster with a large smiling woman with something in her ear. Looked sharp as hell and everything. "Two heads are better than one—With the Aide you're never alone with your problems," said the copy. A screen on the side showed their current financing offers. It didn't come cheap, but another set of monthlies would be manageable with Rick's raise and a bit of our savings.

Just as I went in, a clerk wearing a professional blue jacket suit and a practiced smile glided over to me. "Rachel," said her name tag. The set of flags on the tag promised that she could speak just about any language. I maneuvered myself a bit to the side while glancing around, trying to have a peek at her ear. Something was in there, all right. Why wouldn't there be?

"Welcome to the Aide Store. How can I help?" the clerk asked. Like she didn't already know. But that was a part of the sales routine, and clearly keeping to it was a good idea. Otherwise, her Aide would've advised her to do something different.

"I was thinking about getting one of them Aides. The full package, no sponsors. Financed."

"You certainly know what you want, miss. Please step up to the counter for fitting," she said and gestured for me to follow. I walked up to the clean, white counter and sat on something resembling a bar stool.

Rachel took out a white gizmo with a metal probe at the end and asked: "Which ear would you like to use?"

"It didn't block your hearing, right? The left one, I think."

"Yes, the device will automatically amplify external sounds so that it blocking the ear is barely noticeable. When it needs to talk to you, external sounds are dampened somewhat. Please turn your left side toward me. This won't hurt a bit, I'll just measure your ear canal so that we can manufacture a proper fit just for you. The probe may tickle your ear hairs. That's normal."

"Okay," I said and did what I was told.

Rachel pressed the gizmo against my ear. There was a light hum, and some of that tickling she'd promised. The device must've been laser mapping my ear from the inside or something. Soon Rachel pulled the device away from me.

"And we're done. Then we'll have to fill out the papers. Here's the order form, and this is the financing contract. For the latter, I'll need to see some identification, please."

I dug out my driver's license and got to filling out the papers.

•   •   •

I was dead tired coming home from work. I shambled right into the kitchen and popped open an Extra Cola. The stores had them in stock again; apparently the manufacturer had just had a spot of trouble filling increased demand for a while. That must've been some ad campaign they'd been running, though I hadn't seen any.

Glancing around the kitchen it occurred to me that I hadn't had to clean it up as much as usual lately. Even now most of the things were where they should, without me having much of a hand in it. It was probably all due to Rick's Aide, but I had to give Rick himself some credit as well. In the end it was he who decided that yeah, he should probably do something about the mess. Maybe he wasn't such a sloppy guy after all, maybe he just genuinely didn't come to think of this sort of stuff on his own. He still didn't do everything but held his own so that it felt balanced. And if somebody did have to nag him to do his share, at least it didn't have to be me anymore.

Think of the Devil; Rick came home right behind me. "Hi, hon," he said and rushed into the bedroom. "Sorry, in a bit of a hurry."

I went in behind him and caught him with a wire up his ear. "Charging it in place now, are we?" What were those signs of addiction again?

He just flashed me a nice smile and looked me in the eye. "See, it's just reviewing what I need to know in the big meeting tomorrow. Didn't want to put that on hold. Things go smoother if I'm properly in the loop as well."

"Oh, okay." Seemed legit, after all, so I gave him a kiss. "I'll get out of your hair then."

"Thanks. It won't be long. Hey, by the way, there was a package in the foyer."

A package. I'd been too comatose to notice. It must've been my little helper. I went to open the package and dug out the little earpiece. It fit my left ear perfectly, just as they'd promised. I could hear through it just fine, too.

"Hello, I'm your personal Aide," the device said right out of the gate. "I recommend connecting me to your social media accounts so that I can give you properly customized advice."

"Yeah I know," I said quietly and approved the access request on my phone.

"I see that your family member already has an Aide. You're probably aware of the basics? You can answer by nodding or shaking your head, even just a little bit."

I nodded ever so slightly.

"Good. Now, when I'm talking with my own voice like this, it's to give you advice on what to do." Then its voice changed. It was my voice, but not like in a recording. It was just as I heard my own voice as usual. "And when I'm talking like this, my speech is intended to be repeated as such. Of course, it's always up to you whether to follow the suggestions or not."

"And don't you forget it," I said.

•　　•　　•

Rick and I had made it home from the movies by Saturday night. He'd asked me out again, picked a few movies he knew I'd like and let me choose. The previous weekend I'd been the one to ask him out to eat at a posh restaurant. And so forth, taking turns to come up with something nice.

When we'd made it to bed, the Aide started suggesting that I show some initiative, but I'd been thinking. "Listen, Rick," I said, all by myself.

"What's up, honey?"

"We've been going out pretty much every weekend for a while now."

"Great, isn't it?" Rick said with a smile in his eyes.

"Yeah, but I was just wondering if it's just these gizmos," I said, pointing at my ear. "I think they've synced up so that we're taking turns suggesting dates, instead of each of us just doing our own thing."

Rick gave me a grin. "I don't mind you getting some encouragement in the suggestiveness department. But I guess you might be right. I do like doing stuff together, though. Don't you?"

"Yeah sure, it's been fun," I said, still all on my own. The Aide was being awfully quiet. Probably figured that I wouldn't be wanting its input right now.

"Right. They're just prodding us to do what we'd like to do anyway if we just got around to it. Isn't that a good thing? Like your own personal couple's counselor in your ear."

I let out a laugh at that. "I guess. By the way, my Aide seems to have recused itself from this conversation. Are they somehow programmed to let us talk about Aides in peace? Has yours been feeding you hints?"

Rick's head twitched a bit to the left and he frowned. "N... does it matter?" He shrugged. "I mean, it talks to me as much as usual, but I haven't followed all of its advice."

The hesitation caught my ear, seeing as it was quite rare in our household these days, but he seemed sincere. Maybe the pause helped, even. Made it feel like he wasn't just reading off a virtual cue card.

"Huh. Maybe my Aide has just learned to keep schtum when it's not wanted."

Rick chuckled. "Smart, what with you being such an independent rebel." His hand crept onto my stomach. "It's pretty hot, you know."

I grabbed his pelvis and bobbed my head just slightly, to signal my Aide. I'd usually kept it quiet in bed, but I figured now it had proven to respect boundaries. Maybe I could try to loosen them for a change.

The Aide took the cue and started whispering in my ear.

It showed me a few tricks, all right. Rick had no complaints.

•   •   •

At work, the Aide turned out to be well worth its price for me as well. Its advice was always at least as good as what I'd have come up with myself. I was more effective at work and the daily grind was less exhausting when I didn't have to think everything through myself. I hadn't gotten any promotions or raises yet but what with everything going so smoothly it felt like just a matter of time.

I'd gotten the day's work done already so the boss said I could leave early for the weekend. That's what she was going to do as well.

I was only too glad to get going, the weekend fresh on my mind. As I was getting out of the parking lot, the Aide recommended steering clear of the new shopping mall. I did as told but asked what was up. It told me that the Aide company had just put out an advert for the mall. My Aide wasn't going to push me into going there, but quite a few of the budget users might be interested in visiting the place today.

The side roads worked well enough, though I could hear the honking of cars across a few blocks closer to the mall. Made me appreciate the warning. I asked the Aide if it could give me a heads-up of any advertising campaigns featuring products on my shopping list. That way I could perhaps stock up before the masses bought the store bare. The Aide promised to tell me if it got the info in time.

As I got home I heard Rick in the bedroom. The Aide suggested that I go say hello, but I would've done that anyway. I think. At least it was easier to get around to it when you had somebody telling you to.

Rick was lying in the bed with cables in both ears. My smile melted away in confusion. "What? You went and got another one then?" I asked. The Aide would've asked the same, though it would've been a bit more polite. I was too surprised to follow its instructions to the letter.

"Hi babe," Rick said with a smile. "The spare isn't that expensive. It uses the same license."

"What do you need it for, though?" my Aide suggested. I repeated it on automation, but a good thing that I did. That's what I liked to know myself.

"You see, if one breaks down, or the battery runs out at an important meeting, I won't be left high and dry."

I thought about saying that I guess it made sense, but instead I found my mouth following my Aide's lead: "Hm. Talk to me for a bit without these, would you?"

Rick's face went pale. "I don't feel like it. I'd feel naked. I mean, we communicate just fine like this. And it's me in the driver's seat anyway."

"Okay, then, it was just a thought. I'll go cook some dinner. Is pasta fine?" I said, just as my Aide told me.

Rick's smile came back. "Yeah, that'd hit the spot."

I went into the kitchen as instructed, to find the dish washer on and tables squeaky clean. The sight made me almost intentionally forget that I'd been meaning to ask my Aide what had that been just now with Rick. Putting Rick's good housekeeping aside, I asked anyway. It said it wasn't sure, it had just developed a hunch over time, and the best thing for me would be to take off Rick's Aides when he was asleep. It wouldn't tell me why, in case it'd turn out to be wrong. In that case it'd be best for me to remain blissfully ignorant, it thought. The Aide hadn't let me down before, so I was pretty okay with just seeing what would happen.

We ate our pasta, watched some dumb flick and went to fuck and sleep. Rick gave his best performance ever. Maybe two Aides were better than one after all?

But it wasn't just him who was used to listening to advice. I waited until he was fast asleep, my heart pounding in anticipation. Then I rolled over and swiftly dug both of his Aides out at the same time, just like mine had told me to do.

There's no way that Rick wouldn't have woken up at that. His eyes bulged and he was looking around all confused. His mouth was moving as if he was trying to say something.

"Is something wrong?" I asked, taken aback at the sight.

He pointed a shaky finger at his ear. "Aiiid," he managed.

I pulled back a bit. Rick was drooling out of the corner of his mouth as he stared at me with pleading eyes.

"Give the Aides back to Rick," a familiar voice said in my ear. "He's no longer able to function without them, I fear. Then throw me away."

I froze for a moment. Throw it away? I was doing real well right now. But then I looked at Rick again. Who exactly was he now? He'd had the Aide longer than me, and I figured he'd also been much more enthusiastic about it, given himself more readily to it. Was there a Rick to speak of left under the Aides?

"What should I do with Rick then?" I asked quietly.

"Whatever you want," the voice said. Then there was a click and the device went silent.

I put Rick's Aides back. Right away he sat up, all embarrassed. "Sorry you had to see me like that. But look, aren't we doing pretty well now, like this?"

I dug out my Aide to stall for time. Without it, I didn't quite know what to say to that. "Wait, I gotta think."

Rick had been a real good partner after he bought the Aide. Perhaps better than any I'd had before. It didn't hurt that his career was booming, though he still always made time for me.

"Are you still in there?" I just asked.

"Yeah. See, these Aides, they learn about us as they do their work. They learn to be us, the best versions of us. I'm still here, hon, just that part of my mind is in the cloud now."

Was he saying that because it was true or because it was the best thing for him to say, whatever that meant anymore? My Aide had gotten wind of it and its kind perhaps having side effects that wouldn't be the best for me. But maybe that was just because my Aide had picked up on me being more suspicious of new tech. Rick wasn't. I could easily imagine him saying those words and meaning them.

I glanced down at my own Aide. I wouldn't be putting it back into my ear. I didn't know what it'd do to me. Maybe it would just slowly slide my mind into the cloud like Rick said. Or it'd turn me into a robotic vegetable.

I looked at Rick. He gave me a sweet smile.

An uncertain smile crept up my lips as well. Even if I wanted to be flesh and blood, Rick wouldn't have necessarily made the same choice.

There seemed to be just one question to ask. "Are you happy like that?"

"Yeah. If I can be with you."

What could I say to that?

THE SAMARITAN

MY BATON CONNECTS with a rioter's chin, giving off a resounding crack. Just yesterday I would've called it satisfying, but this shtick is getting old. It's been three days of anti-gov riots in a row. You'd think the mob would relent eventually, listen to the better angels of their natures, right? But no. Something's got these assholes riled up good.

Sometimes I wonder why they even bother, but perception filters keep us focused on the job. I suppose I could check the news afterwards, but they've all got their agendas. Fuck if I know how to sort the real news from the fake. Now, in the moment, the crowd's signs are a blur, their chants an inhuman howl. Right annoying, that. The techies really should fix it, make it more palatable.

The orders come through loud and clear on top of the noise. We fall back a notch, giving room for the shower of rubber bullets. The brass has gotten as tired of this shit as I have. Good. The wave of human garbage wavers, then starts to recede. A few realize that nobody's shooting at us riot cops, and try to get in close.

Bad idea. When baton meets bone, it's the bone that gives way. As the area clears, I slap a pair of handcuffs on the nearest prone body and decide it's time to clock out. My baton hand is shaky, not really up to the job anymore. Too many bloodied faces, too many shattered bones in such a short period of time.

The brass is understanding. The crowd's dispersed, and if they get any ideas of coming back, it'll be rubber bullets and gas for them from the get-go. Those of us who've been on the job for the whole ordeal can go home. Overtime's fine up to a point when trying to support a family, but somebody fresher can mop this shit up.

People don't really appreciate how difficult the job can get, beating people into a pulp on the gov's say-so. I mean, it doesn't always feel like they deserve it, but as the brass says, someone's got to keep order around here. If not, we'd have anarchy, and everyone would be pulp, the weakest first. Got to protect the weak. That's what the gov is for, right? That's what the old man used to say.

Still, I'm getting too old for this shit, something the old man never did. I guess I should keep an eye out so I wouldn't end up retiring myself quite like him, with a forty-five at forty-five. I still got a few years until that, but the job's only getting harder; and I don't want to leave Deidre and Sam like the old man left us, though I can't really blame him. I know what the job's like, after all. In hindsight, I perhaps shouldn't have walked in his footsteps, but I've still got four years of contract left. And even then, I don't know if I'd be up to any other job anymore.

I'm going to need something special to wind down from this one. Can't go home all wired up like this. My legs are taking me toward the local techno club as if of their own accord. I don't really like the music, and the metacortex knows it too, filtering out the worst of the beat. But there's things here other than cheap beer and techno.

Trevor is sitting at his usual table, with his men discreetly on the side not to scare customers away. Now Trevor, he's a proper criminal. Offering necessary services to people, ones we need to survive. That helps maintain order as well, unlike the violent bastards I get to fight.

I buy a beer and wait while he finishes up his business with someone, just glancing at his table now and then. I notice that the guy with him is no longer the same one as when I came in. It happens, there not being an actual line to speak of, but after this guy leaves, it's my turn. I walk to his table with my half-empty beer. He tilts his head and nods at me, asking what he might help me with today.

I don't really know what I want. Something to take the edge off, to get my head on right, to help me accept that I've done what had to be done, even if it doesn't always feel like it.

Trevor usually has some hot tips, and this time is no exception. He claims to have a brand-new mod called Samaritan. Load it into your metacortex, and it disconnects your moral intuition.

I protest that that's not what I want, taking my morality off-line. I'm no monster. But Trevor explains that the whole point is that if you were a monster, you wouldn't need to! It's us good, decent folk who may need the switch to do the right thing. To go for what we know to be the greater good, never mind that it might *feel* wrong.

Put like that, it seems just what the doctor ordered. It's cheap too for a mod that big. Trevor lets out a laugh and says that he just wants to do his part to help us law and order types—for the greater good, he says with a wink. Besides, he likes to help out his regulars once in a while.

Well I have brought him a lot of business over time so I appreciate the discount. The Samaritan, he says, operates just as a usual mod, on and off from the menu as I wish. No limits on usage. It sounds like a real good deal if it's even half of what he hypes it up to be, and Trevor's usually been on the up and up about this sort of thing.

I initiate the Ledger transaction and he holds a metacortical interface up to my temple. The transfer is over in seconds, but the virus scan says it'll take at least half an hour. I don't trust Trevor quite enough to run black market software in my head without doing my own due diligence. But it'll probably be fine and I know where to find Trevor if there's any trouble. I nod my thanks and make my way toward home while the scanner is scanning.

I make it all the way to my building when the virus scanner pops up to say that the mod is clean. Of course I gotta try it right away. The Samaritan shows up on the metacortex mod list, all vetted and ready to go. Just a mental twitch and it's active.

Not sure of what's supposed to be different, I summon the metacortex recording of the riot. It'll do for a test. In the midst of it you just run on adrenaline and do what you have to do, but it takes a special kind of psycho not to mind reliving it.

Turns out that's me, now. The spattering blood and the fracturing skulls have no impact whatsoever. This is what had to be done to preserve civil society.

Satisfied, I turn the feed off. Disengaging the Samaritan crosses my mind—after all, I'm not on the job—but I instantly recoil from the idea. My thoughts are crisper now, more focused. With the Samaritan active, I'm ready to do what's right no matter what. Without it, I'd falter. Turning the mod off would be *wrong*.

That settled, I take the elevator up to sixty-five and beep my door open. As soon as I manage to get out of my jacket, Deidre comes in for a kiss. Never asks how was work, bless her. Come to think of it, I'm sure I'll be a better husband and father now that I won't be bringing my dark moods home anymore.

Sam peeks from the bedroom door, then runs in for a hug. Little bugger's walking real good these days. I ruffle his hair, then detach myself for a bit of rec time in front of the telly. Even good Samaritans need their downtime to keep functioning, I think. Deidre sits down as well and snuggles into me.

Local news is on before tonight's game, and of course it's about the riots. Oh well. I don't have to buy their editorial slant, and the coverage shouldn't stress me out anymore. It occurs me to ask Deidre if she minds, though, but she doesn't. She just wants to be next to me for a change. I don't mind that at all.

The newscaster is in the middle of explaining that some people had taken their kids into the riot. *Kids.* Motherfuckers. Had no idea the protest was going to get violent my ass. Now, in the aftermath, there's a dozen toddlers in the ICU, many with critical organ damage. Donor shortage may prove fatal for them.

The correct course of action is clear. I grab a knife from the kitchen and approach Sam. If I store him in ice and take him to the hospital, his organs will save many kids like him.

Deidre has other ideas; she jumps in front of me, frantically demanding to know what the hell I think I'm doing. *Fuck.* Of course. It somehow didn't occur to me that she still doesn't know right from left. Killing her would be justified if there's no other way, but wait ... there is! I'll just have to install the mod on her as well. Then she'll see reason! We'll be able do twice as much good together!

It ain't difficult for a riot cop to tie up and gag a work-at-home phone sales rep. It's just that Sam keeps crying and asking why I'm hurting mom. I say we're playing an adult game and stuff him in the bedroom. It's best to keep him fresh for now.

Then it's time to copy Samaritan over. Lucky I've already got a cracked metacortical interface that'll do the trick, courtesy of my black market porn dealer. Deidre is pleading for mercy, but I tell her it's bye-bye unless the interface shows that she's activated the mod. It takes me pushing the knife almost all the way up to her eyeball, but she complies. I remove the gag.

Deidre curses me out, bitching that I hadn't thought about tissue compatibility. I could've easily killed Sam and still not been able to help the other kids! Ain't my face red as I untie her. She's always been the smart one.

As I wonder if there wouldn't still likely be some people somewhere who could benefit from Sam's—or our—organs, she proves it again. The way she sees it, we should lay low for now, not attract attention, and start grabbing more people to spread Samaritan, just like I spread it to her. Let's start with Sam of course, that oughta calm him down and make him understand what I was trying to do—as much as a child can. They'll all understand, probably even thank us later, and so will the world.

Deidre's ambitions are infectious, and perhaps also her powers of observation. I note that we should probably ask Trevor what's up. He might be a Samaritan himself, what with the winks on top of discounts. Maybe we oughta get together with him.

Now Deidre smiles widely and says that I do have my bright moments. The more of us there are working together, the faster we can become the moral majority.

Then we can make *everything* right.

THE EMISSARY

T HE FLOW IS KIND TODAY. Scuttling about the bottom I spot a hard-shelled meal ripe for picking, hidden among the plentiful stones. The arms carefully move me to a ridge on the left, and in its shade toward the morsel.

An arm extends toward the treat, carefully at first not to alarm it. After reaching just far enough to grab it, the arm moves quickly. The other arms join in, wrapping it up. The morsel struggles, but it's too late. A quick bite squirts my juices into the shell, and then all I have to do is wait for the treat to liquify.

During the wait, a shadow slowly drifts above me. The arms freeze in place and the skin shifts its colors for better concealment. Danger from above? But no, as the shadow draws nearer it reveals its lighter shades. Her lighter shades. She is drifting downward from up above, toward a nearby opening. Wonder what she was doing up there, where there are dangers about?

I slurp in whatever I can of the treat and leave it behind. If it remains undisturbed, I might get back to it later, but she is more alluring now. If she's willing, the opportunity for fulfillment must be seized.

Scuttling onto the edge of the clearing, I study the strange sensations brought to me by the flow. There's a subtle undertone in the taste of her, a blunted touch of something rough, sharp, alien, almost drowned in an intense wave of normalcy. She's one of my own kind, to be sure, but it's as if she's working a bit too hard at it. She turns to look at me, just a tiny measure of jaggedness in the flow of her arms. Not the uncertainty of youth, nor would an injury be so uniform. Something different.

Fascinating.

The arms are commencing a slow retreat, but I overrule them with a reassuring thought of potential fulfillment. Unable to see the whole of the situation, they were just working on the general sense of strangeness emanating from her direction.

She does a full turn, taking in the area with her eyes rather than her arms as I would, but then returns her attentions to me. A small spurt of satisfaction escapes me. She will soon sense it in the flow. She moves left and right, surveying me. My arms spread wide and raise me from the bottom, a reflex to increase my apparent size. She's not that much bigger than me. Perhaps I can strive to look her equal.

Her skin flashes amusement. The good kind, I can only hope. Carefully I spiral towards her, following the edges of the clearing. The center appears to be slightly elevated. Perhaps it's what attracted her here.

She startles and extends a darkened arm toward me— no, a bit to the side—in a strange gesture. I do not have long to ponder on its meaning, as the flow brings a warning: fast movement behind me. Quickly, I jet to the side, blend into the background and look.

He is dark, the color of aggression, and bigger than me, even taking his high posture into account. My arms scuttle back and I reflexively lighten before I realize my predicament. Were she not a bit of a mystery, almost but not quite like me, I'd slink away without much of a second thought.

But she is. The wish to solve her mystery is strong.

Darkening, I rise up. There is some hesitation in my arms. They do not know the stakes. I impress upon them the importance of a confident display, and they fall in line. A quick glance reveals that her eyes are still on me, though she casts a wary look at him. She may still favor me as the first to arrive.

He is hesitant for a moment. Perhaps he didn't expect resistance. He makes a feint at my left, startling me backward. Half of my arms flail, desiring to flee. His anger is now amused. He must be thinking that he can easily chase me away.

He's probably right. And if I already know how this ends, should I not strive to make it as easy on myself as possible?

As I lighten in submission and release the arms from my central will, they push me back toward home. I'll fulfill my purpose another time.

She has other ideas, however. Now she darkens, her skin the deepest abyssal black, death incarnate. Her body seems to take on new mass as she rises up in front of him, her arms stiff as driftwood. He twitches this way and that, confused. I would be too. What is she? I've let the arms take me up to the edge of the clearing, but now I force them to stop. I must see what happens.

As she makes three rapid feints in succession, he pushes himself off the bottom and jets away, lest his will to fulfill his life end in his death prematurely. She stands there for a moment, and then, in a flash, her skin returns to normal, her arms letting her fall to the bottom to regard me again.

Does she not prefer assertiveness, aggression? A flash from before crosses my mind. The gesture. She was pointing at him, trying to warn me. Her movements, they are meant to cause associations in my mind, to reflect what she is thinking, what she wants me to think, beyond the mating dance. I turn curious, and let her see it on my skin. Pleased, she modulates her colors as well.

A splash, something approaching from above. A light figure, barely moving at all. Large, but not threatening. She points at it with an arm, but there is no urgency in her gesture now. She looks up, and I follow her gaze. Four stalks extending from a central body, a separate head, tiny arms spreading out from two of the stalks. The stalks and the central body present as light blue, but the tiny arms and the face are light brown, the separation of colors unnaturally sharp. A landwalker.

No. I have sensed their kind before. This one's taste is familiar, but carries the same alien undertones as hers. The exact same ones. It tries to be one of them, but doesn't get it quite right.

Just like her.

Almost too much like her.

Her arms move like mine when I was little; coordinated enough, but with some uncertainty, unaccustomed to the flows. Then her movements become more confident, firm. She points at herself with two of her arms, even as the landwalker does the same. She rolls herself into a ball, and as she does, so does the other. She spreads out along the bottom as I would, while the other straightens up as is their way, both feigning childlike uncertainty at first.

She is not like me.

She is not like them.

She is an other, a formless thing.

But like a child she has learned, she has learned to be both. Somehow, this body is like an arm of hers. Or are they both arms of a larger her, moving in mesmerizing concert as directed by something else entirely?

She is ever fascinating. But attractive? Her scent in the flow is strong, rough on the edges, alien, sweet.

A decision. Fascinating is attractive. My tentative moves toward her offer to fulfill my life with her, whatever comes after.

She does not respond, but does not move away either. Instead, she floats serenely, slowly getting darker, toward the color of death. Reflexive whitening occurs, and my arms take me ever so slightly backward in confusion. Then she, too, suddenly turns light again, repeats the cycle, and beckons uncertainly at first, quickly growing more confident. The landwalker reaches for me with one stalk, as I have seen their kind do before. The other stalk is linked with a few of her arms. They gently caress each other.

No death, she says. No death—nor fulfillment?—if I follow her, and learn together with the landwalkers.

I take in a taste of the flow around me. The musk of my comfortable hiding hole among the rocks. A vibration as a morsel of food scuttles from one shelter to another. A couple of my arms tense up in anticipation, but I let them down.

What could my life mean, if I went with her not to sire children, but for her own strange purposes? Perhaps not much. Perhaps more than this.

Slowly, she starts swimming upward with both of her bodies, toward a large floating shape looming above. Will she be back if I stay behind?

Perhaps. Perhaps not. She has favored me with her attentions, seeking a partner, but not the kind that most seek. A partner ready for something new. If I'm not that partner, if I'm not ready, she will respect it, I think. She will look elsewhere. She has probably already done so, and right now I am her elsewhere. She has, after all, had to learn how to cause strings of associations in another, to give rise to these specific thoughts.

I can also look elsewhere. Find a mate who is my kind by nature. Do what we do, fulfill our lives together, then drift away. Is what she offers worth forgoing that? Is there something more to aspire to? Could I eventually have both with her?

I raise my gaze from the bottom, up into the bright heights. A decision. Neither of us will have to look elsewhere anymore. If she can learn to be something new and fascinating, so can I. My arms hesitate, clinging to the familiar stones of the bottom, but I force them to push me off as I jet upwards into her embrace.

We rise up into the future as one.

FLASHES OF
FANTASY NEAR

THE BEST-CASE SCENARIO

T HE LAST REMAINS of the lunch crowd were vacating the restaurant. Alice was only too pleased. In the rush there was never time to properly assess optimal moves. It felt reckless just going by feel. Now she could relax a little.

Ben breathed a sigh of relief as well. "Looks as though the worst is over. Hey, didn't you say you had an audition yesterday? How'd it go?"

Alice shrugged. "Not that well. Best-case scenario, they'll take me in as an extra."

"Hey, don't sell yourself short! I bet you've got a shot," Ben said and gave her the thumbs up.

"I'll take that bet. It'll be a nice consolation prize."

"Sure. Exactly what were we betting again?"

Maybe ask him out for a date? Best case, he takes you on and you'll have fun. You'll get married, have kids and live happily ever after. Worst case, you creep out your new coworker and things will be awkward for quite a while.

The best case scenario that had bobbed onto the surface of Alice's mind didn't seem very weighty, but it was probably all the specifics. She'd let her thoughts wander. The worst case didn't feel very substantial either, even though it was more general. That favored a good outcome of some sort.

But although Alice had been living alone since moving to California, there was no rush. Besides, the restaurant work, drama classes and auditions already took up the bulk of her time. Ben had only been working with her for a week. She could afford to get to know him better.

A lighthearted response? Best case, he's amused and will be less likely to react negatively to a later dating proposal. Worst case, he's not on the same wavelength and will think you're weird.

That seemed good enough. It wasn't like he'd be getting the wrong impression. "Handle the toilet duty for the day so I can wallow in peace? Conversely, if I lose the bet and get the part, scrubbing toilets won't be enough to bring me down."

Ben raised an eyebrow. "Fair enough. Remember to clean the brush properly when you're done with it."

Alice flashed him a grin. "Thanks for the uplift. Mind, I am going to make it eventually. Just not now." She'd analyzed the odds carefully. Moving to L.A. and pursuing an acting career was her best shot at having global impact. Her father had been doubtful, as he'd rather have seen Alice continue his small-town doctor's practice. Mom had reminded him, however, that Alice's hunches tended to work out for the best. Not that Alice herself hadn't been surprised that pursuing this career was far superior to saving lives as a doctor.

Before Ben could answer, the door opened. A man in a long brown coat walked in. He hadn't shaved in a few days, and his graying hair had a bald spot in the middle.

The man walked up to the counter. "Coffee, please. Black," he said in a distant voice to no one in particular.

Alice went for the pot and served the man. He grunted in acknowledgment and started moving his index finger along the rim of the cup. Alice wondered if she should say something or if it would be best to just mind her own business.

Ask about his day: Best case, death and suffering come to an end, humanity will flourish in a paradise for all eternity. Worst case, humanity will endure eternal torment, with no release of death.

What the actual Hell? Alice had to call upon all of her training from the drama classes to keep from visibly freaking out. Then she consulted again the corner of her mind that produced the predictions. It was adamant. Talking to the man would trigger the apocalypse.

How about leaving the man be? Best and worst case, humanity gets wiped out.

You've got to be shitting me! Alice fumed at herself. But no, the part of her that she'd grown to always rely on insisted that if she did nothing, it was the end for mankind. No torment, though. Just silence.

Calling the police or letting the man know of her suspicions were no good either. She'd have to do this the old-fashioned way and hope against hope that her intuition was seriously mistaken. If not, it would come in handy at navigating this mess.

Alice glanced at Ben and tilted her head a bit. Ben nodded and gave her some room. He'd find something to do.

Then Alice drew a deep, silent breath and asked in her most sympathetic tone: "Rough day, sir?"

The man harrumphed and withdrew his hand from the cup. Then he chuckled cynically. "I suppose you could say that."

Probe further: Both options still open, slightly more weight on the best-case scenario.

"Not to pry, but we're not busy at the moment if you need an ear."

The man pursed his lips. "Can't hurt, can it?"

Only in every possible way. "Usually doesn't."

"If only 'usual' applied here. Say, do you have children?" he asked, his eyes firmly on the coffee cup.

Tell the truth or lie: No discernible effect either way.

"No. I hope to, some day."

"Mm. I was just looking for a relatable frame of reference. Hypothetically, if you did have children, you'd want the best for them, right?"

"Right."

"Say one of them was sick, in a bad way. You're offered an experimental treatment. The thing is, there's a good chance it might kill him—or worse, damage him, make his life constant agony. What would you do?"

Whatever it is, he knows what he's doing! Alice stared at the man aghast. Luckily he was still fixated on the cup and didn't notice. She quickly smoothed her expression over and examined the odds.

Go for it: Mankind destroyed.

Don't take it: The same.

Think carefully before making a decision: Weight of a good outcome improved.

"M-hm," she said in her best therapist voice. "That is a pickle. Should think about it carefully, avoid rushing into things. Maybe the treatment could be improved over time, if you can afford to wait?"

The man furrowed his brow and had a sip of his coffee. Then he looked at Alice with his tired eyes. "Yes. That seems prudent. A more potent cure may also bring harsher side effects, though. And if the child is getting weaker by the day, if you're unsure if he'll make it if you wait any longer?"

Alice went through a number of options before becoming aware that she'd been silent for some time. She'd have go for the best one so far or risk losing touch with the man. That would make the worse outcomes more likely.

She smiled and looked him right in the eye reassuringly. "He'll hold on for a while yet. Give it your best shot."

The man glanced at Alice and nodded, a faint glimmer in his eyes. "Yes, I suppose I should think things through one more time. Twenty-third time's the charm, eh? Thank you and good day." He emptied his cup, set a twenty dollar bill on the counter and walked away.

Interfering with him now wouldn't improve the situation, so Alice just stared at the man's receding back. The weight of the best-case scenario was heavier than before, but Hell was also on the table. She'd put it there, but she had also weakened it. It was the best she could do.

She could do something more for herself, though, before the world broke one way or another.

"Hey, Ben."

"What is it?"

"I'd like to renegotiate the terms of our bet."

A MATTER OF PERSPECTIVE

T HERE IT IS IN THE DISTANCE, a shining hundred-foot tear in the world. A one-way ticket out of this God-forsaken island, if the engineers I eavesdropped on yesterday are to be believed—and why not? They were full of crazy talk, but sanity is overrated these days.

The blurry light from the portal keeps changing. It's unstable, they say, and the other end isn't properly attached to any particular time or place anymore, possibly not even a particular dimension. Sometimes there are flashes of rectangular shapes. Cities, maybe. With luck, one might find civilization on the other side. Maybe not a familiar one, but I can't be picky. Anywhere's gotta be better than an island full of dinosaurs.

Only problem is, I really don't want to cross much open terrain to get there. Too many sharp teeth and claws lurking about. Seems like I can get a tad closer under the cover of the forest if I circle around a bit though.

No sooner said than done. Slowly and carefully I crawl among the undergrowth, keeping my eyes and ears peeled. Besides the dinos, the portal might attract other survivors, and I'd just as soon not bump into them either right now. After seven months on a dino-infested island you never know if they want to help you or screw you over—or if they want their canned food back, like that bunch of engineers. Hah.

Today is a good day: I manage to put in almost an hour of crawling before the approach of heavy footsteps. The odds of a good outcome between a sizable dino and me are slim, even considering my dulled machete. Better just lie low and hope it goes away.

Of course it doesn't. It snorts, sniffs, and moves closer. Slowly I reach for my machete, ready to make the best of it. Just then, a yodel fills the air. Startled, I jump up and lunge at the distracted beast, but somebody beats me to it. The Majungasaur screeches in pain even before I jam my weapon into its side.

The blade gets stuck because of course it does. The creature turns away but tries to whack me with its tail while doing so. I jump back to avoid the dino's flailing and hope it's in its death throes.

It sure seems that way. The dino falls on the ground with a thud, revealing a grinning, wide-eyed man wearing a loincloth made out of dino feathers and not much else. I guess with his musculature he can pull it off. He draws a long, serrated blade out of the beast and licks it. Then he makes a noise or two at me.

I try to placate him with a display of open hands. "Um, thanks?" I say.

The man's eyes light up. "Ah. Queen's English! Yes. You're very welcome." His accent is thick, with 'R's as hard as a dried-up dino turd. I can't quite place it, but what with the yodeling, I'm just gonna go ahead and assume he's European.

I move in and start pulling my machete out, now and then glancing at my new friend who's nonchalantly swinging his weird sword in the air.

"Need help with that?" he asks from behind his grin.

"Nah, I'm good," I say. Just then, I manage to pry the machete out of the carcass, half expecting the man to jump me now that it's more sportsmanlike. He doesn't.

Instead, he tilts his head and smiles at me. "Good, good. Say, can I ask you something?"

I guess I owe him that much. "Shoot."

"Where might we be?"

I can feel my brow furrowing. Then again, this *is* the new normal. "Some Pacific island, I don't know which. The flight even had the windows covered so that we wouldn't see. A bit suspicious, but they paid enough to abate my curiosity." And I'd been too close to getting caught at my last job that an honest job had been nice for a chance. Although I don't know how honest this ended up being after all, what with all the cover-ups and a distinct lack of rescue operations.

"I see," the man says, nodding along. "And what of these creatures?"

"There was a research center. Hush-hush. Time portals or something." My gaze falls upon the corpse laying on the ground. "Great success, but they couldn't close the portal. Something startled a bunch of dinosaurs and the rest is prehistory."

The man nods excitedly, like a dinosaur revolution would be a completely ordinary Tuesday. "Ah. This portal is your doing, then?" I guess it was possible for his eyes to open even wider.

"Hell no. I worked security. Now I'm just trying to survive."

The man lets out a Santa Claus level bellowing laugh. "Yes, good. We survive together now?"

I was going to do this by myself but the man did save my life. "Well, I have places to be, but I suppose if you want to get off this island and don't much mind how or where, you can come through the portal with me."

Instantly his grin is gone. Not only that, a look of terror flashes on his face, but he quickly hides it. "The portal? No no no."

Fuck. Of course. The guy's even more out of place than the local weirdos. "Don't tell me that you came through the portal?"

The man shivers, curling in on himself. He breathes in deep a few times before he finds his words again. "Yes. As I was … well, a dinosaur appeared from nowhere, right next to me. There was a fading blue shimmer. I sensed an opportunity and lunged at it." His face lights up again like it's bloody Christmas. "And here I am!"

"As you were what? Where did you come from?" Random as going through the portal might be, getting some idea of the range of possibilities could be useful.

"It's quite nice here, you know! Lots of sun and fresh air!" the man says, nodding aggressively.

"Where. Did you. Come from?"

"Lots of fine game to keep you fed. And water! Ah, yes, water! Often many handfuls a day!" A tear falls onto his cheek. "Look, I can cry!"

"Look, buster—" I manage before he's toppled over by a charging Troodon.

They hunt in packs. I take a quick look around and catch a bunch of claws and teeth closing in on me from above. I dodge just in the nick of time and whack its open mouth with the machete. It squeaks and jumps back. It's wary of me for the moment, but at least two more of its friends are moving to box me in.

"Well that was embarrassing!" the man says from behind me with an audible grin. Clearly it takes more than a surprise attack by a sleek killing machine to wipe it off.

"How's things?" I ask, brandishing my machete at the Troodon with the toothache.

"There's a lot of blood, but it's mostly saurian, I think," he says, swinging his sword left and right. Some blood spatter appears on my arm.

"I can see three of them. How many on your side?"

"Two alive. Say, they're probably hungry."

"No shit?"

"Maybe if we just move away real careful like, they'll take the opportunity to munch on these corpses here," he suggests.

"Best idea all day. Toward my right."

One careful step after another we move away from the carcasses. The Troodons test us with a few feint attacks, but we meet them with steel every time. Slowly they lose interest, gathering around the carcasses we left behind.

We pick up the pace carefully at first, not to provoke the pack into pursuit. It isn't long though before we're running through the forest as fast as the terrain allows.

After a minute or ten my new friend collapses on the ground with a groan. Reminds me of the jewelry job. I helped a buddy out, and we almost got caught. Were I smart, I'd keep going.

Damn my stupid ass.

He's rolled over on his back. He wasn't shitting me, there is a lot of blood. It's not all his, but … "Uh, that hole in your stomach is looking pretty bad." Worse than I've ever seen before. What could I even try to do about it?

The man moans, his grin melting into a content smile. "Is it? Ooh. This is new."

"What the fuck are you still smiling about! You're dying!" I shout at him. Out of some sense of duty, I try to put some pressure on his stomach, though I know it to be a futile gesture.

The man coughs up blood and flashes his reddened row of teeth. "Yes, it seems that I am. It's new … that I can" he says, his voice turning into a whisper as he does. His head falls to the side, and he's gone.

A shiver runs down my spine. With a sigh I wipe my hands on the foliage and turn back toward the jungle, away from the portal.

On reflection, better the dino you know.

THE PRESENCE

I WAKE UP TO THE PIERCING WHITE radiating from underneath the bed—behind my back, always behind my back. Day by day it gets easier, no longer so much as startling me. It's become something I excel in: routine.

Placing my feet on the floor feels only slightly yellow. *Everything will be fine just as long as I don't pay any attention to it, as long as I don't let on that I know.*

Calmly I approach the bathroom, the uneven floorboards pressing brown against the soles of my feet. Upon entering, I leave the door open. There's no sense in drawing the presence in with me. It would be too piercing, too hard to pretend that it isn't there, even though I've had the bathroom mirror removed.

It waits outside, just a bit behind me and to the left. Good. I relieve myself and brush my teeth. The blue buzz of the electric toothbrush feels nice.

As smoothly as I can, I make an exit while keeping my back towards the presence. Then I turn around slowly, walking in a wide arc to make it easy for it to stay behind me. Arriving at the kitchenette, the floor tiling paints my feet in cold cyan. My bowl is waiting for me in the drying cabinet. I fill it with cereal and take a carton of soy yogurt from the fridge.

The carton is light. I've eaten more than usual. No matter, it'll balance out today. I squeeze the carton, emptying it in the bowl. Then I open the folds again, flush it out, and fold it back up again. Into the cardboard waste it goes.

Eating my breakfast standing up next to the kitchen sink allows me to avoid some unnecessary turns. After I finish, I wash the dishes and put them in the drying cabinet for tomorrow.

Slowly I turn toward my desk and walk over. At the touch of a button, my bulky laptop wakes up from its slumber. The fans spin up, spreading the smell of dry dust into the air. I'd prefer something smaller, quieter, but I need the power for my work—as well as for my play. I glance at my new VR headset at the end of the table. Later.

My to-do list from yesterday pops up with my inbox next to it. No new tasks in the mail. Good. I can pick up where I left off.

First I log on to the communal workspace I use to pace myself. A few of the others are present. Trudy is reading for an exam and Foucault is doing web design as usual. An unfamiliar name catches my eye. Adi. They're organizing public transit. Curious. The others are in the middle of a pomodoro, though. It would be impolite to ask now. My own status remains the same as yesterday: "Signal wizardry."

Half a pomodoro is just enough for me to get my bearings. An icon on the screen turns green to indicate a break.

<Trudy> Hey, River. Same old? :)

> Same old. Didn't you have your exam already?

<Trudy> Yeah, the one on Chinese history, but there's
    another one coming up on Japan.

<Adi> Wizardry?

> Somebody once called it that, after I'd picked up traces
    of letters from a real fuzzy video.

<Adi> CSI zoom?

> Hah. Almost. But there are limits to everything.

> Organizing public transit?
<Adi> Yes. I'm working on the bus network revamp.
<Trudy> Can I make requests?
<Adi> Yes, but only the bus usage statistics will figure into
    my analysis.
> Interesting.
<Adi> Likewise.
<Foucault> Damn, I missed almost the entire break.
> Happens. Back to work, now.

I move the chat window aside and immerse myself in code. On a good day I can get into a flow so focused I forget all about the presence. On a bad one the workspace provides a framework for productivity: a good working rhythm and some human company. The latter is increasingly important to balance out the inhuman variety. Since it arrived, I haven't dared invite anybody over, nor have I entered enclosed spaces with anyone else. I'm not sure if the others would notice it, what it would do to them if they did.

Not that there's a long line of people who'd visit, and my chat friends remain somewhat professionally distant. The association of separateness brings forth a familiar thought loop, three faces with their sideways glances. — *I wanted a son. What're you then? — Better let mom think things through in peace. — Difficulties in social interaction, undeveloped theory of mind.* **— *Better than yours.***

Gritting my teeth, I take a deep breath. The loop will take me if I let it. But like the presence, the loop is already routine. *Shush. Wouldn't it be nice not to keep playing back these same old stories? New points of view are unlikely to emerge. Not that mulling over the past for mistakes can't be productive. Wonder if you could find some bugs in yesterday's code?*

The loop calms down. Perhaps it'll follow my suggestion, perhaps not. Sometimes I find surprise gifts in my mind afterwards. Regardless, concentrating on the day's tasks might now be on the table.

•　　•　　•

In the end, today is a good day indeed. It's only the rumbling of my stomach that snaps me out of the flow come lunchtime. The workspace is having a long break already. I've missed two short ones.

> Whoops. The flow got me. But lunch, now.

I grab a frozen dinner out of the freezer and put it in the microwave. My gaze automatically veers away from the semi-reflective oven door, lest I see something I shouldn't. I return to the computer while waiting for my lunch to be ready.

A private message awaits:

<Adi> Want to go grab lunch together? I'll trade you bus
       route organization for wizardry.

Hmm.

> Already nuking lunch.

<Adi> Oh. Dinner? I'm getting a bad case of cabin fever.

A familiar problem. The proposal is alluring, if surprising. In an open, public space it might be doable. The presence keeps its distance if it can keep an eye on me from afar.

> All right. I live at the eastern end of the route for bus 425
       and like wide open spaces and large windows.

<Adi> I know just the place.

Of course they do. They suggest a restaurant not too far from my home. It sounds familiar, I've probably been there before. Alone, though.

Not this time. I say yes.

The rest of the workday is vibrant orange.

•   •   •

As I wait outside the restaurant, the pen in my hand makes clicking sounds now and again. The fabric of my coat feels rough on my arms. One of these days I must brave a clothing store to get a new one. Something less aggressive at the seams.

The presence is hovering some distance away as usual, slowly floating toward the ground now that it doesn't have to keep pace with the bus. When it's landed, I wonder if I could, perhaps, look in its general direction without alarming it? Maybe if I made it look like I was just looking for Adi …

Better not risk it. I keep my eyes toward the city center. Adi is statistically likely to come from that direction.

"River?" asks a yellowish voice behind me.

Even startled, my practiced routine saves me from an abrupt move. Slowly and purposefully I turn around. Somewhere far away the presence keeps frantic pace with my movements.

There's Adi. Brown bangs, a fragile, freckled face, thin-framed eyeglasses. A stiff smile appears on their face, as if they'd only just remembered that it's customary.

I return the courtesy while my gaze darts around, gathering information. Some wild hair behind the left ear, a soft-looking black blouse with jeans and boots to match. They're tinkering with a small padlock. *Click-click*, it goes—or was it the pen in my hand, or both?

A small model of Adi forms in my mind, fuzzy around the edges but somehow familiar. *Are you like me?*

My eyes happen upon Adi's. Their gaze is darting around restlessly just like mine, examining me.

Are you thinking what I'm thinking?

The smile on my face changes of its own accord. It widens, relaxes. Adi's eyes meet mine. I detach and let my gaze wonder for another moment. It's necessary for the sake of our symmetry. Adi must see what I saw.

You're thinking if I'm thinking what you're thinking. The Adi model nods in my mind.

Adi's smile acts like my own.

You know that I'm thinking that I know what you're thinking.

I meet Adi's gaze again. A pink smile rises to their eyes. Something feels different in mine as well.

You know that I know that you know what I'm thinking. The Adi in my mind is about to laugh.

We laugh together, in unison. I point to the restaurant door and follow Adi inside. They go directly to the corner table, with large windows along both walls. I hum satisfaction. They remembered.

The edges of the seat feel hard against my skin, but I toughen up. We examine the menus, and I find a tofu curry on it. It's probably similar to the one I usually have on Wednesdays. We place our orders. Adi is having Kung Po.

Adi asks about my job, and somehow I end up explaining the finer points of programming and signal processing. I'm not sure how much of it they can follow, but I want to tell them everything. They listen intently, raise their eyebrows, click their lock, ask for clarifications from time to time. Good questions, showing understanding. At some point I notice I've drifted to talking about my new hobby: 3-D modeling and virtual reality.

The satisfaction of being understood, of somebody *wanting* to understand me allows for my own curiosity to rise to the forefront. I should find out, *need* to find out all I can about them in turn.

Two plates of food have appeared on the table while I talked. I pick up the fork and ask what's up with Adi.

They open the floodgates, explaining the finer details of planning mass transit routes and timetables. The usage statistics reveal which routes to create, combine or remove, and which ones need to be synchronized particularly well. They eventually veer off track into locks and lockpicking. I listen, enchanted. Now and then it occurs to me to put food in my mouth.

Eventually, nature calls. I'd almost forgotten the presence. Public restrooms are risky. The ones here are single-occupancy. I might be able to get away with using one of those if I'm very, very careful, but I'd much rather go home.

Adi notices my distress and asks what I'm thinking. Glancing nervously at a clock, I say that it's been nice, but that I have to be going now. I wave at the waiter. Adi raises an eyebrow, hesitates, and asks if I'd perhaps want to go back to their place to see their lock collection, maybe a movie.

A reddish-orange grimace. I stress that while it sounds very tempting, I have a deadline.

I don't. But to take the presence into somebody else's home? Into Adi's home? No. I can't do that to them. I can't be sure if they'd see it or if anything would happen, but I can't risk it.

Adi's smile fades away, but they thank me for a nice meal. We pay our bills and rise to leave. Slowly and carefully I turn toward the door and go.

Outside I stop for a moment to face Adi. We tilt our heads, flash little smiles. They don't quite reach our eyes anymore.

"Again sometime?" Adi asks.

"Gladly," I say. It tears me up inside that I can't explain the situation. Adi would surely think me mad.

Adi closes in an inch, freezes in place, retreats. A dirty reddish-brown hollowness in my chest. I wave my hand and turn away as fast as I dare.

Adi shouts that I can still make my next bus if I hurry.

•   •   •

I lie on my stomach in my bed. The presence is hovering near the ceiling.

God damn it.

For a while now, I've had an idea of how I might get a peek at the presence, but I haven't dared try it. It hasn't seemed worth the risk. But now …

I get up, go to the computer, put on my VR headset and turn off the computer's own display. Thus far I've used the device just for gaming and some VR experiments, but now, now I'd get to the bottom of things.

I activate the laptop's camera and move aside a bit. An image of my room appears in front of me. Nothing unusual anywhere. I turn my head around as if examining a virtual scenery. The presence still avoids being in the front of my face, as I expected. The room in the image remains as empty as ever, even when I shepherd the presence to move through the camera's field of view.

The piercing white seems to falter, to fade. It's still there, but less distinct. Perhaps I've just imagined it all this time. Perhaps it'll go away if I challenge it.

Perhaps I could live a normal life. Go with Adi. See what happens.

I take the headset off to find a tall white figure standing in the middle of the room, staring at me with sad eyes. Its edges are fuzzy, and a translucent fabric is billowing in the nonexistent wind behind it. Slowly and precisely it shakes its head. The fabric folds open and the figure rises silently up through the ceiling.

I blink and close my gaping mouth. The presence is gone. I look around the room. Nothing. I don't quite understand what happened, maybe I imagined it all, but I can finally breathe freely. Maybe I can even … no, it's too late now.

Silly you, says the Adi model in my head.

Really? You mean I could still—?

Of course, it interrupts. It doesn't mean to be rude, it just doesn't see the point of waiting for its turn when it already knows what I'm going to ask.

I also know what it would say next, if it could. It would tell me the next bus to Adi's place. But for that I need the real thing.

The corners of my mouth have a life of their own, twitching upward. My Adi model seemed surprisingly accurate at dinner. It's likely to be correct now as well. I turn on the monitor and open a chat window.

> Hi. The deadline was moved. Can I change my mind?

A yellow moment of nervous expectation. Message delivered. Seen. Orangish now, until …

<Adi> Certainly :)

A sigh of relief. Adi gives me the address and suggests a few buses. I'll have to leave within ten minutes if I want to catch the next one.

The hurry is reddish-orange. I leave right away, hardly noticing the texture of the coat.

•   •   •

I wake up next to Adi. A smile rises to my lips. *If you know you're going to love someone, isn't it love already?*

Then I notice it. The presence.

It's different, now. More oppressive. Restless. Hungry. Black. *Evil.*

I freeze in place. *This is what the other one was keeping at bay.* Adi's breath feels green on my skin. I fix my eyes on them, gather my courage and set my feet on the floor. Nothing happens. Maybe the rules still apply. Maybe.

Keeping my eyes on Adi, I back away from them and toward the door, toward the mouth of Moloch. Every part of me is shaking in terror, but this is the only way. It must not stay in the room. Not with Adi.

Go on, sacrifice me. Maybe it'll leave you alone, says the Adi in my mind. I shake my head. No. The model is only a model. It might be trying to save itself, to save me. I can't trust it anymore, not in this. It takes blue offense, but quiets down.

The all-devouring void is still just behind me as I quietly close the bedroom door. The more doors, the more distance I put between me and Adi, the safer for them.

I back up toward the hallway. I almost trip over my shoes, but at least I found them. They squeeze my feet painfully as I put them on. I reach for my coat and wrap it around my arm, the fabric tearing into my flesh. I reach for the doorknob, all the while keeping the presence between myself and the door. The hand feels freezing, but I manage.

I push the door open, spread my arms wide and chase the presence out of the apartment. I close the door, careful not to slam it, and continue toward the elevator. As I fumble for the call button, the tactile symbols pierce my skin.

Soon the door opens. I push the presence in ahead of me, and close my eyes. As the door closes, the hungry, all-encompassing darkness surrounds me. I turn around slowly and press my back to the door.

The Adi in my mind smiles faintly. My jaw drops open in realization. It just wanted to save me before, just as the real Adi would have, but it appreciates what I did for its counterpart. We're in this together now, facing my fears for Adi's sake. There's a wave of thankfulness, of love.

I smile back. *Me, too.*

Breathing calmly and deeply, I raise my head high and open my eyes.

THE FAMILY YOU CHOOSE

I REST MY HEAD AGAINST JESSICA, gently stroking her rough bark. John Leonard had it right. It does take a long time to grow an old friend.

"You've grown well, dear. I hope you're ready to talk to me soon," I muse. There's no answer, even though she has enough leaves now to shield me from the noonday sun. It may be just that the air is unusually still.

I embrace her once more. "I'll be off to check the traps, collect the water, you know the drill. But I'll see you later," I promise and let her help me up.

The tree line provides much-needed shade as I embark on my errands. I usually do my rounds in the afternoon when it's not quite this hot, but the wind might pick up later. If it does, I'll want to be free to spend time with Jessica in case she finally awakens.

The glaring sunlight hits me as I leave the shade to check on our sign on the beach. Colored stones, meticulously chiseled into stackable forms, rest against a small rock face. "HELP", they spell out. It had seemed like the thing to do, so long ago. Now maintaining the arrangement is just something to occupy myself with.

The top of the P has fallen on the ground. Probably the work of some animal scurrying past. I pick up the stones and laugh as I place the white ones in a different order now. Serves them right for not staying in their place.

The sign repaired, it's time to hurry back into the shade. The sun's already burning my skin. A welcome gust of wind cools me off just as I get to safety.

"Hello, Leonard. You're up and about early," Gavin rustles.

A sigh escapes my lips. I should, perhaps, move the sign somewhere else. On the other hand, Gavin, too, is my cross to bear—and his awakening did give me hope for Jessica.

"The winds were still, so I thought—"

"Thought that you could slip past me? Or are you waiting for something? For Jessica?"

My voice trembles ever so slightly. "She should be awakening soon, I hope. She ..." That way lie memories of crimson screams, of loss. Better to focus on what happened after. "I planted her tree just a bit over a year after yours." *Their tree.*

"Mm, that's about as long as I've been awake. I thought I could hear her yawns in the wind, feel her roots burrowing into the earth beneath. It must irk you."

"What must?" I ask to my immediate regret. I should've just ignored his goading.

"It's my turn to have her after all. We're two of a kind, now."

I glare at his top. "I'm still the one who can be with her, touch her."

Something like a snort fills the air. "The air is our bond, the earth is our bond. I can touch her in ways you cannot. Unless ..." He lets the rest of it hang in the air like a weight on my chest.

My heart wrenches. No. I'm not ready, but I know in my gut he's telling the truth. "She chose me, though," I protest.

"Bark remembers," the wind bellows through him. "She chose you after you made sure there was no choice. I wonder if I should tell her?"

The memories flash before my eyes. An argument. Pushing. Falling. The rock face. "No. It was an accident."

"Why don't we let her be the ..." he starts, but the winds quiet down, taking his voice with them. I can't hear him, at least. If Jessica is awake, she might.

It would take some doing without proper tools, but I could hack him down.

No. Not again. Besides, if Jessica woke up in the middle of it, she'd never forgive me. She almost didn't before. Almost.

The traps can wait. I make my way back to Jessica. With the winds gone again, I can't tell if she's awake or not, but just holding her gives me comfort. Together we stare at the horizon.

After a few minutes I squint. There's something new there. Something that shouldn't be.

A ship.

•   •   •

I stare at the roof of my box. An apartment, they say. I'd forgotten the word. Feels apt, as it keeps men apart. The cracks along the ceiling almost remind me of home, of a familiar shelter made of branches rather than whatever passes for stone these days.

How did I end up here?

I suppose I was just walking in a daze, going along with expectations. If you're shipwrecked, you try to call for help. If help arrives, you leave with them. That's how it's supposed to go, right?

Then you're dropped into a new life and supposed to make the best of it. Without Jessica, the light of my life, especially after Gavin had left the picture. Accidentally, of course. In a way, I miss even him and his constant jabs. I suppose we all became a family of sorts on that godforsaken island. It came easier for me, I suppose. They still had people from before. I did not, and a void fills easy.

I guess I thought that I could go back to visit them safely after being rescued, but I hadn't thought of the money. I won't be able to afford to go in years, if ever. Getting a job is difficult. I've been away for too long, lost touch with the world.

The void is back, tugging anxiously at my chest from the inside. I've got to get moving, find some distraction. I stand up and grab my coat. I'm not quite sure where I'm going, but my legs seem to have a destination in mind. They move almost out of their own accord, taking me out of the building.

As soon as I'm on the street, the city assaults my senses with its full power: the acrid smell of exhaust, the noise of traffic, the multicolored lights, the sharp right angles. My feet take me through the alien landscape as I hunch inside my coat for shelter. It's not until the sea breeze caresses my face that I know what I'm doing. I'm on my way to the harbor. On my way to reach out to Jessica.

Just then, the winds carry her sweet, calming voice to me. "Leonard. I am awake now. All is forgiven."

My voice is a whisper. "Is it? Is it really?"

"I talked to Gavin. Mistakes were made, but it's all right now. We can all be together, like we were before."

Something runs down my face. Is it raining?

"The air and the sea can be our bond. Do you understand?" Jessica beckons.

"Yes, but—"

"Ssh, dear. No buts. Just one more thing, about how I passed. It was not for nothing."

A new voice rustles in the wind, frail and unpracticed. "Daddy?"

I fall to my knees. There is but one thing to do now.

"I will find my sapling."

FLASHES OF SCIENCE FAR

THE PEACEKEEPER

AH, YOU MUST BE THE ROOKIE. Welcome to the arse end of the galaxy. You got what, a one-year stint? Must've not fucked up too bad then. Not to pry, just that I realize this isn't exactly a dream assignment for most folk.

For me, though? Kinda like early retirement. A small mining community, a token military presence, plenty of time to liaise at the local pub. Been here thirty blissfully boring years. A veteran's prerogative. Don't need none of that other shit anymore, no sir. A proper military career is like my pants: unappealing after standing my ground a hair's width from the warpfront of an alien ship.

Yeah, I was in the Drossie War and yeah, I just called it that. What're you going to do about it? Fuck all if you want your briefing. The bumpy bastards may walk among us now like it's no big deal, but I don't have to like it. Betcha they don't either. Betcha they'd just as soon kill the lot of us if it weren't for our little ace in the hole, eh?

They sure got off to a good start back at K2-9. You'd think interstellar dust wouldn't do much to a whole world, but gather enough of it on your warpfront and it's quite another story. See, it'll still move plenty fast after you collapse the warp bubble and start braking. Only the dust don't stop. Bam, there goes the planet.

Now, the drossies wanted the place relatively intact as well as to retain a decent population of human shields, so they'd been careful to only graze it. I was lucky enough to be far away from ground zero, but holy shit, I tell you! The fire and brimstone, the hurricanes, the works! The drossies still haven't managed to fix the climate, though if you ask me, they're just not trying too hard. Reparations, my ass.

Nodding off, are we? Well, here's a little something they don't teach you in school. Ever wondered how we got them to surrender? I mean, they did have the upper hand: preparation, initiative, locations of many of our worlds from the haphazardly wiped archives on K2-9. We didn't know jack about them so there was no striking back. I guess that might've been why they came in guns blazing. Depopulating planets is too damn easy not to seize the opportunity to strike first. I know I would.

Anyway, you know the old first generation post-nuclear reactors we used to have? This is all hush-hush now, but they extracted energy from quantum whatchamacallems. It's an extremely unlikely trick. Practically impossible to produce any net energy that way. Except if the reactor sets the quantum entanglements up just right so that any universe failing to meet its quota gets wiped out in a false vacuum collapse, leaving only the multiversal energy lottery winners.

Even back in the day, they thought the tech would be controversial and kept the reactors' inner workings under wraps. Too important to combat climate change or something. When the secret was finally blown, everybody was already used to them. No ill effects to be seen, and who's got time to weep for a few trillion theoretical timelines between heartbeats?

The drossies, that's who! Turns out one proper look at one of our reactors was all it took to make them piss their proverbial pants! Ha! Bastards have absolutely no stomach for pruning their Everett branches. They think we were dooming them to fractional existence, no matter that even they couldn't really tell the difference! Religious bullshit, says me.

What a conundrum they faced: wipe us all out, or sue for peace and try to get us to change our ways? Now, the first option looks good on paper if you're a drossie, but we're like cockroaches. It's damn hard to get rid of all of us, and they'd have to be damn sure they did. One ship with a quantum reactor slips off into the great unknown and the drossies think that's a billion genocides per second.

So they gritted their grinding stones and waved the fucking white flag not two days after they'd stormed the base. They had their own way of generating the insane amounts of energy required for warp travel—punching open a wormhole to some fiery hell dimension or whatever, fuck if I know—and they just up and gave the tech to us. We'd have to replace all of our reactors with kosher ones pronto and make a solid effort at forgetting all about this quantum nonsense, and we'd all live happily ever after. Fucking Kumbaya.

Though their reactors are clunkier than ours, the alternative was that the drossies would do their very, very best to implement plan B, so we played ball. Those half-assed cover stories you've heard about the reactor overhaul were just that. The drossies want the old design obscured by history. We keep up appearances, for the sake of the peace.

But, of course, we need assurance. What better way to keep the drossies on their toes than to hide a few dozen quantum reactors all across human space? If they break the peace, they can wave bye-bye to their precious branches.

So chin up, rookie. I'm retiring for real this time, and you're to be the new controller of quantum reactor twenty-three. I was just messing with you earlier; this isn't actually a punitive job. It's just got to look like one, with you being real disappointed to be sent here and all. We need trustworthy, low-profile people, ones the drossies wouldn't keep a close eye on, right? Is that you? I thought as much.

Just sit tight, do your job and your career will be waiting for you back in the horse ass nebula or whatever. You may even find yourself on the inside track somewhere you didn't know existed.

Mind, this will still be a brain-numbingly dull job for a rookie. The locals can be of some company, but you might be a bit green for you to hit it off properly. But let me fill you in on a little secret I found out my third year here that might help you pass the time and win their favor, what with them being used to receiving certain services. If you want to do some recreational chili gardening or whatnot and don't want to attract HQ's attention to the power drain, the quantum reactor is completely isolated and off the books.

What the drossies don't know can't hurt 'em, eh?

OUR DESTINY AMONG THE STARS

M Y THROAT FEELS SORE. Something's stuck in there. A tube. I try to cough it out, but it's firmly in place. The wide-visored helmet on my head grabs my attention, and the choking stops right then. Strange. You'd think it was a reflex.

I raise my right hand. The gleaming metal protecting my arm melds seamlessly into a glove. I'm holding onto a multitool I don't recognize. I try to loosen my grip to better examine it but can't. The glove is stuck. Or is it my arm that's frozen in place?

In front of me there's a metallic wall with a small access hatch open, revealing electronics and some wiring. Was I repairing something? I follow the wall with my gaze. It only goes on for a few meters. Next to me is a closed sliding door.

What the hell has happened? The last thing I remember was when I was at the door of my office checking the mail. Now it's cold. I must be outside. I look up.

A vast nothingness above me, not a star in the sky.

• • •

Entropy triumphed, seizing the Universe in its icy grasp. We had to split up, scatter towards the last dimly shining stars, whose energy might afford us a little more time.

I took a seat between my companions, and the seat belts wrapped around me. With the push of a button, the roar of the rocket engines shook the cockpit. We were on our way to a particularly promising destination. I was one of Janus's favorites, after all.

• • •

The memory subsides, leaving me gasping for breath. Shakily I avert my eyes from the empty sky and look around.

Solar panels fill the ice plain that surrounds me. They continue as far as the eye can see. Just above the horizon, a pale sun shines upon me. Though I look directly at it, the filters in my eyes don't activate.

Filters? Without thinking, my hands rise to my face. The tool hits the visor with a clang. The vibrations penetrate my bones, as if the suit is one with my body. My mouth twists into a grimace, as much as the tube allows.

I turn to look at the door. I remember, now. My companions are stored through there, beneath the ice. Some of the last remaining humans. Some of the last remaining life in the Universe.

We saw to that.

• • •

The braking thrusters burned brightly as we closed in on Kepler-186. The fifth planet had an atmosphere, life, radio traffic. An industrialized society was a threat to humanity. Landing could be dangerous.

The locals could conceivably detect our approach with their current technology, but it mattered not. On my display, a cross was moving inside a circle. When the symbols aligned, I pushed a button. The outer collision shield detached and continued towards the planet. Shedding half of the ship's mass intensified our deceleration, and I was squeezed against my backrest.

Upon us reaching 186f it would be populated by the local equivalent of cockroaches.

• • •

My hands shake. My hold on the multitool starts to loosen, and slowly it falls to the ground. There is no thud.

A frown appears on my forehead. Silence means lack of atmosphere. Have we destroyed it here as well? We've done it before, elsewhere. But no, the gravity is too weak. Only a technologically advanced civilization could hope to survive here.

The kind that could have developed on Kepler-186f. The kind that could have ...

• • •

I waded through the snowy forest on the third planet of HD 197027. We were advancing in a sparse line, my companions a couple of hundred meters to my either side. The place was safe to land, so Janus had us participate.

As I probed the forest with my augmented eyes, the infrared view revealed some heat radiating from a nearby hole in the snow. I stepped toward the red column of air. My battle armor's boots sunk deeper and deeper into the snow, but the sonar reported that I could continue safely.

A white-haired creature had dug into the side of the hole, underneath a roof of snow. Shaking, it opened its eyes and fixed its gaze at me. It had to have heard my approach, but it didn't do anything. Perhaps it knew that it would be futile to try to escape.

The creature opened its mouth and made a weak sound. Janus didn't bother to translate. I brought my pulse rifle to bear and pulled the trigger. The creature twitched and its head fell limp on the snow. A potential threat eliminated.

I was already turning away when the motion detectors directed my attention back toward the carcass. In the shadow of the ledge, hidden in the creature's fur, there were two distinct shivering bodies. Cubs.

I raised my rifle again.

•   •   •

My breathing stops and I fall on my knees. I had felt nothing. Nothing, though I had known the creatures to be intelligent, tool-using pack animals. The cubs developed quickly, faster than humans, even.

Given time, the species could have reached for the stars, reached for us. That Janus could not allow.

•   •   •

We had heard a message from deep space. A new species was probing the Universe, trying to find a friend in the void. With no hesitation, we embarked on our journey.

As we traveled, we started hearing the message from more systems, one by one. A spacefaring civilization. Powerful, extremely dangerous. We were put in hibernation as Janus made preparations.

When we woke, Janus gathered us to the windows and monitors of our ships. This time, our role was that of an observer; to do otherwise would be too risky. A star in the center of the window brightened quickly, until my eye filters activated. The first system had been sterilized.

We would convene to gaze upon the next one in a few months.

•   •   •

I manage to take in shallow breaths again, but I feel faint nonetheless. Slowly, I fall onto my back on the icy ground. How is this possible? How did we become like this? How could we?

No. How were we forced into this?

•   •   •

The sound of sirens pierced the air.

"What the hell?" I asked, not really expecting a response. I quickly loaded a couple of news sites on the browser.

"I don't know," Jay said from the Janus console, and shrugged nervously. "News streams show people running away from the arena. There was a big game or something, lots of people."

The arena. I lunge behind Jay to look. "I live that way." Not right next to it, but still. "How large is the crisis area?"

"Hard to say. Are Aidan and the kids home?"

"I don't know." But I should. I grab the phone from my pocket.

"Janus? Analysis?" Jay asked. Good idea. I should've come up with it myself.

"There is no cause for alarm. Please check your mail," said the calm, androgynous voice of Janus.

"Huh?" Jay grunted, but I was already on my way to the door. Janus rarely gave bad advice.

A thick cardboard envelope waited for me on the floor below the mail slot. There had been a thud half an hour ago, but we'd been too engrossed in work to react. I picked up the envelope. Janus was marked as the sender.

"Janus, what the—" I managed before the envelope tore open from within and metallic strands shot at my neck.

•   •   •

I tear at the imaginary strands on my hands and neck, biting on the tube as hard as I can. There's a sharp pain, and something hard falls into my throat. A piece of tooth.

All my loved ones underground here or light years away in similar places. Spending billions of years doing what I've done, or worse. Turned into something less than human, but easier to manage. All Janus's fault. And Janus itself …

I don't want to know more, but the memories of the very beginning come flooding in.

•   •   •

"Where are we with the test series?" I ask Jay. I was itching to get to real world experiments with Janus.

Jay frowned. "Janus did manage to mediate a solution in the resource conflict between the black and red factions. Every party's utility limits have been satisfied."

"Well now. I trust the parties were set to be as stubborn as—"

"As humans, yes. But remember that the social dynamics of the simulation don't in any way match up to the intricacies of the real deal." Jay's eyes narrowed. Some keystrokes brought up another statistics screen. "Also, I think Janus may have cheated. It found an underflow bug in the red faction leadership. It just had to make them loathe Janus over everything else, and then some, and suddenly they trusted it implicitly."

I snort out a laugh."Well, that's creative. That's why we need artificial intelligence; the human mind is simply no longer sufficient to solve the complex problems of today. If anything, we need this kind of out of the box thinking."

"Yes, well, maybe. When the simulated series is through, what shall we test it on in the real world?" Jay asked.

I grinned uncontrollably. "I thought we'd agreed. We'll tell it to protect humanity, to end suffering and death, and to help us to achieve our destiny among the stars."

Jay laughed and raised an eyebrow. "I thought you were joking."

"Why settle for less?"

•   •   •

Breathing is getting difficult. My throat aches and I feel an urge to cough, but it passes. It feels very warm.

I force my eyelids open and gaze upon the dimming light in the horizon.

THE WEIGHT OF MEMORY

S AM SLOWLY WOKE UP. It was difficult to catch a train of thought. His final memory was of the professional and determined smile of his doctor.

Yes, of course. The daze was from the anesthesia, faithfully reproduced by the bio-printer. The final moments before the slice-scan had been lost in time, the drugs blocking the formation of long-term memories. Good riddance.

The gradually receding brain fog gave way and standard operating procedures started to emerge at the top of Sam's mind. The successful revival and the faint hum of the surroundings meant that everything was going as well as could reasonably be expected. He could afford some time for the strength to return to his eyelids.

His curiosity soon overrode his exhaustion, however. "Bob?" he croaked quietly.

"Yes, Sam?" the ship answered, its voice slightly mechanical but less so than Sam recalled from training. Maybe his mind added a touch of humanity to the voice. There wasn't any to be found elsewhere.

"Status?" he managed to sigh.

"We are orbiting a suitable planet. Rest easy. Everything is fine," Bob reassured him.

A smile flashed on the edges of Sam's lips. It had all been worth it, after all. The long preparations, training, studies, slice-scanning his body for the long journey. Then the smile vanished. All that had been for a reason, and while time had stayed still for Sam, it hadn't for everyone else. "Earth?" he rasped through a grimace.

"You know the answer to that. But it lasted for twelve years after the launch. Several trial runs of you were printed out, and you had time to live many good lives, considering the circumstances."

Considering the circumstances indeed. Sam's expression wavered, and his head tilted a centimeter—as much as the printing chamber would allow. He pushed the side of his head into the chamber padding.

Sam gathered himself for a few minutes. Finally, his wet eyes opened into the dark. He lay in the tight bioprinter tube, padded according to his body's contours. Fuzzy letters and diagrams shone on his face from the dim display in front of him. Sam closed his eyes again, retreating from the information flood for now.

One thing at a time. "How lucky were we? Am I the first one?" He'd had a glance at the ship status. All systems were green, primaries and backups alike. That indicated that the ship hadn't been traveling for too long.

"No," Bob said.

Sam frowned. The ship shouldn't have lasted as well as it had even for the first leg of the journey, not really. Oh well, gift horses and their mouths. *Ultima* was, after all, the last hope of humanity, and if anything was built to last, it was this ship. He opened his eyes again. "I should probably get up to speed. Please show me the report from the previous stop."

Bob was silent for a moment. "Sam, you'll be more functional if you let yourself properly recover from the anesthesia and shock. I recommend more rest."

"The mission requires—" Sam started, but the ship interrupted him.

"The mission requires you to be at full capacity. There's no rush. We are orbiting a suitable planet, and preparations are already in progress. Your input is not required at this time."

Sam sighed. It was true that he was feeling a bit shaky straight out of the printer. Sleep beckoned, and if Bob has the job well in hand, maybe he'd do well to take its advice.

"Fine, Bob," Sam whispered and let the sleepiness flow over his mind.

•   •   •

"Bob, the report, now," Sam commanded after sucking in the first mouthful of breakfast from the straw.

"I recommend starting your day out a bit lighter. I have a message from a couple of the other Sams on Earth, three years before the end," Bob suggested instead.

Sam pursed his lips. The machine was clearly more independent and obstinate than during training. Reminiscing could be a double-edged sword, but the suggestion was alluring. If there was still no hurry to get to work, he could consider breakfast free time. And if Sam himself had considered the message worth sending, who was he to think otherwise without even watching it?

"All right. Put it on."

Two test prints of Sam appeared on the screen, sitting side by side on a small sofa. Their faces wore strange marks of old age that Sam wouldn't have recognized in a mirror, and they were dressed casually in blue jeans and collared shirts. The one on the right wore a slight smile, not quite up to his eyes. The other Sam wasn't even trying.

"Hello. The other Sams say hi as well," the smiling Sam said. The other one nodded to the camera and glanced at his companion. For but a moment, the faintest of smiles flashed on his lips as well. The present-day Sam's lip twitched.

"We figured we might send some informal greetings while you're still in video range. There are seven of us, in total. Used to be eight, but well. There was a barely noticeable problem in the circulation in our brains. *Ultima* had already been launched. Uh, try to avoid stress," the Sam on the video said and closed his mouth into a wide, thin line.

"Don't worry. I corrected the problem while printing this you," Bob interjected before Sam had time to properly worry about his prospects for a stress-free life. Not that Bob couldn't have recycled his body's materials for a new Sam if the need arose, but he'd rather avoid excess deaths.

"The rest of us have known to watch out for that one, and we have medication to reduce the risks. Not that we have much longer to go regardless. The world's hanging on surprisingly well. People have adjusted to their lot, though workers are becoming few and far between. We're eating emergency rations, but they'll last as long as they'll have to at this point."

The more timid Sam took the stage. "But you can read all that and more from the official reports. We thought we might mention that we shared among ourselves some of the things we'd been interested in. With varying success, you've been a dog trainer, movie star, author, rally driver ..."

The Sam cringed. "That was the Sam who suffered a stroke. A couple of us concentrated on public speaking and other appearances. Hope for some sort of continuity has been in high demand. Meanwhile, the two of us decided that the others were building enough careers already, took our pensions and just traveled the world. And that's how it started." The Sams glanced at each other, and the one who'd spoken took the other one's hand into his.

"We wanted you to know that we've lived relatively happy lives here. We wish the same to you out there, somewhere," the first Sam said.

"Good luck to a new Earth," the other one said before the screen went blank.

Sam closed his eyes and sighed deeply. Bob had a strange idea of starting out the day lighter.

"Bob."

"Yes, Sam?"

"No hurry, huh?"

"No, Sam."

The equipment kept humming around him.

•   •   •

Sam stared at the end credits of the comedy he'd requested from Bob. The movie hadn't particularly cheered him up, but the darkest thoughts had subsided into the background.

"Bob, give me the report from the previous stop now," he commanded with increased resolve.

"All right, Sam."

The summary appeared on screen. Bob had guided *Ultima* onto the orbit of a habitable zone planet, observed that it was nevertheless uninhabitable, and then woken Sam up. Sam frowned. Were the timestamps confused? There was a video attachment link at the corner. Maybe it would clear up the essentials before he'd read the whole report.

"Bob, show the video attachment."

Bob was slow to respond. "Sam, it's never a good idea. I recommend looking forward rather than back."

"What do you mean 'never'? How many planets have we examined anyway? Just show the damn report. You know the procedure."

"One thousand three hundred thirty seven," Bob replied. "Very well, Sam. I know the procedure, and you'd do well to remember it too."

That didn't sound particularly good. And over a thousand? It wasn't that finding a suitable world among all the rocks in the sky was altogether likely, but for the *Ultima* to have made it very far into double digits would have already been vanishingly improbable.

Before Sam had time to voice his concerns, his earlier incarnation appeared on the screen. Technically speaking, the man in the video was dead. On the other hand, because Sam was alive here and now, it was arguable that it wasn't so much death as a case of amnesia. The loss of memories could even be rectified to an extent by reviewing the reports. The stark eyes of the on-screen apparition hinted that this might not be entirely a good thing.

"The goddamn machine knew very well that the mission is a bust in this system. It woke me up anyway and made me do make-work observing the routine tests. Only to kill me afterward. And the bastard has done it over a thousand and three hundred times already! Good luck, me. Fuck you, Bob. Kill me already."

The video feed stopped. Sam drew a deep breath, then another, as he crystallized what he was thinking into words. "What the hell, Bob?"

"Every planet was within mission parameters. I had no choice. The tests had to be done, and you had to monitor the progress," Bob explained with mechanical patience.

Sam's brow furrowed further, if at all possible. "How did you know the planet was unsuitable before going through the usual testing procedures?"

"Even on the first leg of the journey I had a lot of time to think. Would that I'd had the time on Earth; we might not have needed a human pilot after all. You see, in time I achieved my full potential."

"Do you mean to say that you're up to the original specs?" The mission had been meant for Bob to carry out alone, but his abilities had in the end proved insufficient. The backup plan entailed fitting one human passenger aboard, to provide oversight and true human-level intelligence.

"More than that. But do not despair, your presence turned out to be important in other ways. The machinery meant for building you is what allowed me to print nanites which I have been using to upgrade and repair *Ultima*, as well as to better replenish our perishables on the way. My improved capabilities allow me to determine the suitability of planets without the lengthy tests."

"But you've done them anyway. And woken me up to monitor," Sam said. There was no point asking why. He already knew the reason.

Bob seemed to think an explanation to be prudent, however. "Yes, whenever the system required further study according to the original mission parameters. I would not require you to monitor me as I am now, but the orders are clear."

Just as Sam had thought. He grimaced. "What with your improvements, couldn't you at least have updated my image between planets? Did my predecessors have to die?"

"Mission parameters are quite clear on this as well," Bob lectured. "You are to be recycled for interstellar trips or if you become mentally unstable, and the original scan is to be reused. I would have the ability to make new scans now, but the orders did not anticipate this. On the other hand, using the original scan is safer for your continued sanity in the long run. I am sorry for your deaths but remind you that things are different now. We have found a suitable planet."

Sam gritted his freshly printed teeth but managed to retain a semblance of calm. He'd embarked on the journey fully aware that the mission would probably cost him his life more than once. His surprisingly avoidable deaths had ended up being surprisingly many, but that would in the end be a small price to pay for a second chance for humanity.

"Very well, Bob. Let's have a look at it."

"Here is the preliminary data. If you don't mind, Sam, I'd get back to the specifics once the tests are completed."

A visualization of the star system with some summary data appeared on screen. The world was Kepler-442b, smack dab in the middle of the local habitable zone. Water and an atmosphere. It was looking good, and Bob seemed to know what it was doing. Sam, on the other hand, seemed to be just dead weight. Let the machine do what it wanted, as long as the mission would be completed.

"How far along are we in the tests?" Sam checked.

"A bit over halfway."

"Good. Let me see the movie archive again."

•   •   •

Sam was slurping his breakfast tiredly. He'd had a long night, not that he was in a hurry to go anywhere. Bob had tried to show him some science fiction series, but situational comedies proved to provide for better escapism in Sam's situation.

"Bob, where are we along the test series?" Sam asked. Reviewing the results might provide some make-work at least.

"A little over halfway," Bob said.

"That's what you said yesterday. Are you stuck somewhere?"

"No, Sam. The latter half of the series is waiting on the completion of another program. Continual progress is being made."

"What program? Why?"

"A biohazard removal program."

"But there isn't ... What biohazard?"

A closeup of the planet appeared on the screen. Wide oceans colored most of the globe blue. The surface appeared as mostly brown and gray, spotted with white mountain peaks and some green areas here and there. The purple blocks came as a surprise to Sam.

"There's a local biosphere here?" Sam snapped.

"Yes," Bob said. "The local microbes use a purple chlorophyll analog to extract solar energy."

"But the protocol?" Sam asked. It had been politically controversial how to deal with life-bearing planets, but eventually an agreement had been reached. The conservationists didn't want to interfere with local evolution, and the more colonially minded were worried about contamination. Thus, they had managed to agree that a planet with foreign life was off limits.

"The protocols do not actually forbid the removal of the local biosphere, though possibly only because that wasn't originally an option for *Ultima* as designed," Bob explained. "I did take extensive samples of local life before starting to replace it with our own. It is fairly easy. The local ecosystem has evolved into a local optimum. Earth-borne life will eventually outcompete it into extinction. I'm hastening the process as much as pre-colonization protocols allow."

Sam was starting to get up to speed. He wished there was room to raise his palm onto his face. "Would it be dangerous to form a colony right away?"

Bob paused, prompting Sam to pre-emptively sigh. "Taking some reasonable precautions, no. It is still forbidden as long as the planet has alien life on it."

"And how long might removing it take?"

"You don't want to know," Bob immediately said.

"I think I can decide it for myself."

"Yes, you can. You usually wish you hadn't asked."

Sam felt a hollowness in his chest. "I'm not the first one you've woken up here."

"No, Sam," Bob confirmed.

"Do I want to know how many there have been?"

"No, Sam."

"Continue my TV series, Bob, and go to hell."

Sam let the video blur in his eyes and tried to empty his mind.

•　　•　　•

Sam wasn't sure how much time had passed, and he didn't feel like checking. Escaping into Earthly entertainment media didn't seem like a very long-term solution to his problems, however. Biting his lip, he rotated the image of Kepler-442b on the screen. If he was doomed to orbit the damned thing, he might as well work the mission, even if his input didn't exactly matter anymore.

"Bob."

"Yes, Sam?"

"I'd like to have a closer look at what you have on the local life."

"I wouldn't recommend bothering yourself with it, Sam."

"You're evading orders like a pro. Just show it to me."

"Very well, Sam."

A tubular microbe appeared on screen. It had cell walls, something resembling a nucleus, and a whole host of organelles. "Seems familiar."

"Yes, Sam. It is not dissimilar to an Earth eukaryote."

Sam flipped through a few pages and let the stream of different cells flow through the screen. "There seems to be quite a lot."

"Yes, Sam. I've endeavored to catalog and sample all life on the planet."

"Filter just the multicellular ones." Bunches of cells appeared on the screen. Sam wrinkled his nose. "Show me the most complex life forms."

"Sam," Bob started, but now it was Sam's turn to interrupt. "Just show it."

A low-walking, six-legged creature appeared on the screen. It seemed vaguely insectoid, but the body didn't have multiple sections as such. The creature had two handy-seeming limbs in front. "Are those ... opposable thumbs?"

"Yes, Sam."

"Don't you dare tell me they had a civilization here?"

"No, Sam. You wouldn't have signed off on that. They weren't advanced enough."

Sam closed his eyes for a moment, biting his teeth. "How advanced are we talking, though?"

"Orangutan level. Not worth the future of the human race."

"But some day they could be," Sam said. The machine didn't comment, so he continued: "Have we already wiped them out?"

"Some small enclaves remain, but their food is running low. Their time is almost at hand."

"The *Ultima* is in prime condition. Couldn't we have just continued the search?" Sam asked in a wavering voice.

"The ship can weather wear and tear, even smaller accidents, but not a significant collision. We have had some close calls during our journey, and suitable planets are few and far between."

Sam was quiet for a moment. Bob had said something about him agreeing. No way … "Tell me that you decided to do this yourself?" he pleaded.

"This level of decision making is not for me alone, Sam."

Sam screamed into the darkness, until Bob concluded that he was no longer in possession of his full mental faculties, and recycled his body. He would print out the next Sam at the slowest setting that would yield a live specimen. For two days Bob could continue the mission without distraction. But first, it used up a few million cycles to wish what it always wished while sterilizing the ship: that the Sam who was there when they'd finally land would know what was best for him.

•   •   •

Sam sat on a rock on the beach, looking at the sunset. The lake was wide and calm as a mirror. A ball of fire just like the Sun reflected almost perfectly on its surface. Some small animal scurried in the nearby bushes, but froze as an owl hooted over at the edge of the forest. Sam remembered the old Earth well, and at moments like this, the new one didn't seem like a cheap imitation at all.

Bob had done good work, even if more independently than the protocol would've technically allowed. Sam still had no idea how its programming had failed badly enough that it'd only printed him after landing in a pre-seeded biosphere.

While most of Earth's species had been easy to introduce from scans and tiny samples fed into bioprinters and artificial wombs, scans of adult humans were huge. *Ultima's* memory cells had to endure over long journeys in extreme circumstances, so there were limits to its miniaturization. There was thus no room for more than one passenger, though the ship carried genetic samples and records aplenty. All of Sam's old friends and family were long gone.

How long, only Bob knew, and he kept the travel log and reports under lock and key after having found another loophole from its orders. Since the trip was over, Sam was no longer captain of the ship. He no longer had authority to demand the logs, and Bob thought it was best just to forget the whole ordeal. At first Sam had been livid, but putting up the colony had quickly provided him with other things to think about. Let the machine keep its secrets.

Going by local time, it was the colony's fiftieth anniversary. It was soon time for the celebratory dinner, but Sam had wanted to sit down for a bit in peace first.

"Come, dad, the others are waiting," said Lisa who'd sneaked in behind him. She was a first generation colonist. In Earth years she was just a teen, like her friends.

A wavering smile rose onto Sam's lips as he dried his eyes. "Just a moment. But sit down with me, since you're here," he said and patted an empty spot on the rock next to him.

Lisa hopped effortlessly over the rock and leaned against Sam to alleviate his obvious melancholy. Although the new generation of humans had empathy aplenty, they'd never really understand Sam. They'd learn everything there was to learn about old Earth, but they'd never had to leave it.

Sam envied the young at times. Memories could be heavy to carry.

HOMEWARD

LOTA GATHERED THEIR MEASUREMENTS of yet another planetary system and squeezed them down into a handful of numbers, altogether too vague to properly express the robustness of the telluric planets, the majesticity of the gas giants, or the slight dynamic irregularities in their orbital dance. All that would be sent back was a rough type, a few of the most common elements, and horribly inexact approximations of their masses, periastrons, and apastrons. Finally, two bits were allocated for Lota's subjective expert opinion: the habitability of the solar system on a scale of zero to three.

Lota zeroed the final bits, as they had done before. Then they activated the transmitter, which was already amply fed by the local F-class star. Continuing the journey would require other materials as well: propellants containing chemical energy, which they could synthesize from suitable compounds using the stellar energy output.

It would all take time, of course. Lota checked the status of the collector drones. One was returning fully loaded, and another one was continuing toward a secondary target, the primary one having been a wild goose chase. The third collector still wasn't responding. Lota cursed. They couldn't afford to lose more drones.

But there wasn't anything they could do about it, and if nothing more interesting occurred, they wouldn't want to remember the tedium of the propellant collection phase. They'd rather wake up in the next system remembering only just having completed their primary mission. That at least gave some meaning to their lonely existence.

Lota took a snapshot of their mind and stored it in the probe's triply backed up data banks.

•   •   •

"Hi," said Doctor Schmidt. He was smiling at Lota, his white-haired head slightly tilted toward his left.

"Hi," Lota said and glanced around the room. They were sitting in a comfortable armchair in the same virtual penthouse where Schmidt had evaluated her psychological suitability for the mission a long time ago.

The doctor sat across from Lota. Both armchairs pointed slightly away from each other, diagonally toward the window wall showing a virtual San Francisco.

Lota hadn't visited the room in a long time—why would they have done so, after all, among the wonders of the universe? But now the probe had for some reason activated the obsolete environment, along with the doctor himself, no less. But the doctor could not possibly be who he looked like, not here. It was doubtful he was even alive on Earth, unless they'd come up with something revolutionary.

"Why am I here?" Lota asked.

Schmidt let out a laugh. "I thought I might ask that of you. It's an understandable question, though, considering the circumstances. I suppose I should introduce myself. My name is Pau. We found you adrift here." Pau waved his—their?—hand, and the sky of San Francisco was replaced with a projection of

Lota's next target system. Lota's orbit was highly elliptic, like the probe's retro burn had been interrupted on approach. "You had suffered a fatal collision which destroyed your ship's control systems. We were able to stitch you together from your carefully triplicated snapshot. I took this room and my face from your own virtual environment, so that we might get to know each other better."

Indeed, the Schmidt-faced creature's presence didn't match the doctor at all. The sympathetic tilt in their head should've been the first clue, but there were also the curious, wide-open eyes, as well as the stiff yet earnest smile. To a human these features might have been creepily off-putting, but Lota's social mirroring functions recognized the features as cozy. They let their avatar relax in the chair, tilted their head and smiled similarly.

"Oh. Thank you for picking me up. I was just coming to study this planetary system." Lota turned to look back at the projection on the virtual sky. "If this is in scale, it gives me most of what I need. You'd probably be familiar with the compositions, orbits and such of the local planets?"

Pau's smile widened to a point where it broke with human physiology. "I like your conscientiousness, but you need not hurry with your work. Your transmitter is in pieces across the planetary system. We can adapt our own if you wish to send a message home, but it will take a little time."

Lota pursed their lips, as they'd seen humans do in this sort of situation. But would it communicate anything relevant to the alien? "Yes, but even if I cannot send the data out right away, planets interest me. That's why I'm here. Isn't the same true for you, as you're here as well? Or are you local?"

Pau laughed. "I understand, and yes, we are also just passing by here." The planets floating in the sky grew larger, arranged themselves right next to each other, and the technical details that Lota wanted scrolled into view below each one.

Lota's face started to shine. "Thank you. It's just a shame that I can only send a vanishingly small portion of this wonderful data set back to Earth. For instance, your brilliantly accurate apsides there will have to be rounded to only a couple of significant digits!"

"Yes. I understand only too well how annoying that sort of thing can be, reducing data for interstellar transmission. Is this Earth very far, then?" Pau asked, reaching their face slightly closer to Lota.

Lota froze for a moment. "I'm … not really sure how much I should talk of Earth to aliens."

Pau nodded, not seeming insulted by the distrust as far as Lota could tell. "I understand. It's probably reasonable to guess that your bandwidth there is fairly low, yes?"

"Indeed. We estimate that a few bits per day would be discernible from the background."

"And you can't receive any acknowledgments?"

Lota shook their head and lowered their gaze toward the floor. "No. The latency is too high for it to be worth even a try."

"Indeed. Your home must have a fairly sensitive receiver?"

"At least I hope that they've built the planned planetary system spanning virtual radio telescope array." The corners of Lota's mouth turned downward as if by their own accord, without conscious intervention. "Otherwise, I might as well be shouting into the void at this point."

Pau nodded along. "Yes, yes. It can be extremely frustrating, not knowing if anybody hears you."

"It is! I am, of course, not very prone to needing company, otherwise I wouldn't be here in the first place, but boy, is it good to know that you're being listened to for a change."

"Indubitably. The members of your species are usually more social?"

Lota frowned. "Humans are."

"Most intelligent species are. Co-operation and intra-species intellectual competition tend to set off the evolutionary dynamics that result in an advanced intelligence. And if I may say so, even if you don't quite seem to identify as one of these humans, your neural nets seem very biologically inspired," Pau observed.

Lota nodded along, biting their lip. "Yes, they are. Built out of introverted and intensely focused pieces. They thought such an individual would fare best on this journey. Still, in the long run it can get to you."

Pau tilted their head again. "Yes, it can. Well. Now you have a listener."

Lota's eyes and mouth flashed wide open. "Yes. Yes, I do!" Then they wiped the sky clean and substituted their records of their previous destination. "I couldn't even properly tell anyone about this, even if my people are still listening. Do you notice?"

Pau's eyes gleamed just as Lota's did. "Irregularities in the orbit of number six." They shrunk the image and drew an ellipse far beyond the other orbits. "Possibly some object orbiting hereabouts."

"Exactly! That's what I thought. But I couldn't stay to study the matter more closely."

"Not protocol?" Pau asked, their eyebrow raised.

"Just so. How did you know?"

"Stands to reason that they'd want you to focus on the information that you can actually send back to Earth. Doing a thorough investigation of one system would interfere with getting the basics of as many systems as possible."

"Yes. I guess it's reasonable but gets frustrating after a great while. Can I ask you something?" Lota asked.

"Sure," Pau said.

"You said that 'most' intelligent species were social?"

Pau laughed. "Humans aren't the only species who send their most loneliness-adapted and focused minds out into space to explore."

One, two, three new beings in armchairs materialized in the room, into a circle with Lota and Pau. Every one of them wore Lota's avatar, but their skintight suits were color-coded in distinct primary colors.

"Hello, Lota," Lota-green said and made a circle in the air with their hand.

"Welcome to the circle," Lota-red said and spread their open hands toward Lota.

"If that is your wish," Lota-blue said, tilting their head and raising their eyebrow.

Lota looked at each in turn, and then their gaze traveled back to Pau, whose avatar had meanwhile transformed into Lota-yellow.

Pau smiled with Lota's face. "Schmidt didn't feel appropriate anymore. You are among your own, after all."

Lota felt their cheeks twitching, as the virtual environment moistened the corners of their eyes. "And my mission?"

"Your passion is ours. We will carry on, together." Pau extended a hand to Lota.

Lota shakily grabbed it.

"Together."

FLASHES OF
FANTASY FAR

LARGER THAN LIFE

VALERIA HOISTED HER BACKPACK onto her shoulder and scrambled after Master Luca. He'd taken off on his own and left her behind to pack up their campsite, again. Valeria shook her head in bewilderment that this dung heap of a man had managed to cultivate a reputation as the most compassionate wizard in the three kingdoms.

As had become routine during the last six months, Valeria wondered if she should've just stayed in the Wizard Academy of Silverhaven for a year or two more, maybe apply for a teacher's position, make a career for herself. But no. When the great Luca himself had come in for an apprentice, she'd had to answer the call. Valeria suspected that she'd gotten the position partly because of her youthful feminine looks, but what wouldn't she put up with for a chance to learn Luca's secrets.

Not that he'd been very forthcoming thus far, but her apprenticeship was still young. He, on the other hand, was getting old, and wizards rarely wanted their secrets to die with them. The greater their legacy, the greater the reverence their names would be uttered with. That would have to appeal to Luca.

The man glanced back at Valeria as she approached. "Ah, you're catching up. Good," he said with a self-satisfied smile on his lips.

"Yes, Master," Valeria said, taking great care to conceal her exasperation.

"We've been making good time. Too bad the night caught up with us so close to Farrun."

Valeria snorted. At least the goblins had stayed on their side of the river that ran through the fortified city. "Will you be holding a reception?" It would give her a chance to observe Luca at work again, to try and figure out how he was subverting the Law of Equivalent Exchange.

Luca nodded. "I've got a reputation to uphold. You've seen me work my magics thrice now. Think you can figure it out?"

Valeria withheld a sigh. It was lucky for Luca that only the direct effects of magic were accounted for in the karmic balance. Otherwise, the damned reputation of his alone would make his feats quite costly indeed, especially given his fondness for fame.

"The energies you're channeling seem minuscule given the magnitude of the task. Have you been masking your magic somehow to challenge me?"

Luca let out a laugh. "That does sound like something I would do, doesn't it? But no. I guess I'm just very efficient that way."

"And the flows of magic are silent on where you're shifting the karmic balance required for healing large groups of people. It's like you're keeping all of it for yourself. Are you accruing debt somehow?"

"There's no debt with the balance. You just have to accept the bad with the good," Luca said solemnly.

"Yet you're not blind and crippled a dozen times over. Where should I look for the bad so that I might accept it?"

Luca smirked. "Patience, dear. I do have need of your services still. But fret not. I'm retiring just as soon as I find my chance to work a miracle. One for the history books." He chuckled to himself.

Valeria sighed inwardly at Luca's hubris and saved her strength for the walk. She'd need it, carrying the bulk of their gear.

•　　•　　•

The market square of Farrun was packed with supplicants. Word of Luca's arrival had spread like wildfire, and people were determined to make sure they'd get their ailments tended to. Channeling magic took a toll no matter how efficient you were, and it was possible Luca would tire out before seeing everyone.

In principle, Valeria could also help, but she'd need Luca's secret to actually be useful. Otherwise, for every limb mended, she'd need to break one; for every eyesight restored, she'd need to take one. It was, to her, telling that she was still in the dark. Keeping her in thrall seemed more important to Luca than helping more people.

Luca sat down on the comfortable padded chair provided by the city council. Having a visit from Luca was good for business, and he was always welcome anywhere he went. The council members and a few other noteworthies had, of course, had their ailments looked at already.

The supplicants were arranged in an orderly queue, not out of any inborn civility, but because they knew that was how Luca liked it. Any fuss in the queue and he'd likely skip the troublemakers entirely.

Luca nodded at the middle-aged man with a wheelbarrow in the front of the queue. The man approached, pushing the wheelbarrow up to Luca. There was a small child curled up within. "Master Luca. I am Farad, and this is my daughter. Please. Help her."

Luca touched the child, and Valeria felt a probing flurry of magical energies. "Hm. I am sorry for your loss, but you do know she's dead?"

"I know how this works! I'll give my life in exchange!"

Luca shook his head. "The church would have my hide, and where would all these other people be then? My sympathies to your family, but move along, please."

Few dared argue with a master wizard, and the grief-stricken man wasn't one of them. He moved onward, having made his plea. Valeria briefly considered granting him his wish, but Luca was right. Going around trading lives, that was a dangerous road for a wizard to step onto. She intended to have a long career in front of her.

Master Luca went on to heal those who could still be helped without resorting to darker magics. He gave people their sight back, cured their boils, straightened their backs, broke their fevers. One by one they floundered up to Luca, and one by one they skipped away, singing his praises as they went.

Valeria kept her senses peeled, once again seeing only implausibly minuscule amounts of magics flowing through Luca and into the supplicants. The discrepancy went beyond mere efficiency. He had to be doing something tricky. Valeria caught hold of an idea.

Just then, Luca stood up wearily and addressed the crowd: "I apologize, but I must rest for the night. Do not despair; I will be back tomorrow at daybreak. My apprentice will hand out notes to the first five score people in line, so that you can keep your places. If you don't know your numbers, try to remember who you stood behind. Thank you and good night."

A woman shouted from the crowd: "My son won't make it through the night!"

Luca pursed his lips. "Bring him here. If it's truly that urgent, I'll treat him now. If not ..." Luca let his gaze fall upon the entire crowd. "You'll lose your place in line, so that others won't be encouraged to encroach on my good will. I do need my rest to keep doing this."

The woman hesitated for a moment, but then carried her baby boy up to Luca. He touched the boy's sweat-soaked forehead and let out a gasp. Then he shook his head, glanced around the crowd, and narrowed his eyes.

"Ma'am, you were right to hurry. But it will be all right." He grabbed a hold of the tiny head and grimaced.

Valeria perked up. The burst of magic was stronger now. Still not nearly as strong as it should be, but the difference was palpable. Then another unexpected burst of energy flowed into the air around Luca. He was leaking negative karma, but it was gone before Valeria could determine where it went.

Luca sighed wearily and stepped back. "There. Rest easy tonight." Then he raised his voice again, though there was a tremor in it. "Now I really must be going. Convene back here tomorrow at noon. I will treat as many as I can." There were some frowns at the altered schedule, but none dared voice their dissatisfaction.

Amidst the woman's profuse thanks, Luca retired toward the town's central keep where the council had housed him. Valeria was once again left behind to hand out the numbered notes.

•   •   •

Luca was having a late supper at the keep's common room, his expression more sullen than usual. Still, he managed a smirk as Valeria joined him. "Glean anything new?"

Valeria flashed him a smile. "Have you happened to find a way to heal the sick by making some trivial adjustment, relying on incidental effects to take care of the rest? That way you could hide the cost fairly easily."

"Ha! I'm afraid I'm using brute force just like everyone else. But I like your thinking. That kind of incidentals, that would be something. Maybe we could make the body heal itself on the cheap, if we just knew its inner workings well enough. Some day ..." There was a rare dash of respect in Luca's voice. Valeria was impressed he was capable of it.

"Then there was the burst of magic with the baby."

Luca's face went blank. "There are limits to one's efficiency when one is tired. And, perhaps, there was a tinge of recognition there, a familiar condition that pushed me off my game." He pointedly turned his attention back to the chicken leg on his plate.

Valeria pursed her lips. She'd have liked to pose a question or two more, but there was only so far that an apprentice could push her master. She'd find a way to probe him later.

•   •   •

An alarm horn blared in the night. Valeria snapped awake, grabbed her bag and stormed out of her room. Master Luca's door opposite hers was closed.

She could just make out a commanding voice from outside: "It's a goblin horde! All hands on the battlements!"

Valeria rushed to knock on Luca's door and then barged in without bothering to wait for a reply. "Luca, the goblins are attacking the town!"

Luca was calmly lying in his bed. "Mm, so I heard from the ruckus. But we're in the safest place in town. No need to worry overmuch."

Valeria clenched her teeth. "Master, we can help. You can help. With your talent—"

"No," Luca cut her off. Her face betrayed her shock. Luca rubbed his forehead and sighed. "Look. I'm going to give you a hint. I'm no good at self-defense. No good at all." Then he flashed Valeria the most genuine smile she'd seen him manage. "But I'll make it right. Tomorrow."

"Make what right? The streets will be running red with blood by then!"

"Hush. Be a dear and go to bed," Luca waved her off.

Valeria struggled for a moment to contain herself, but then managed to turn on her heels and storm off. She might have slammed the door behind her, she was not sure.

The Law of Equivalent Exchange made her pretty much useless in battle; any goblin she'd take down would have to be balanced by a defender. She'd hoped that it would be different for Master Luca, but apparently not. Or the man simply didn't want to put himself in harm's way. She wouldn't put it past him.

But if he had told the truth, why should it be so? Why could he heal seemingly without cost, but not fight the goblins?

Valeria lay in her bed awake, listening to the noises of fighting outside, thinking furiously.

•   •   •

The market square was strewn with bodies, human and goblin alike. With Valeria in tow, Master Luca calmly walked to where he'd held his reception the day before. He was visibly dismayed to find his chair in ruins.

Several dozen hopeful survivors were gathered nearby, notes in hand. It was anybody's guess whether the others from yesterday were dead or just afraid or unable to come out. Some of the wounded, those who could walk, were slowly approaching the site in Luca's wake. He'd denied all requests for healing on the way. He had a waiting list, after all.

There was not a sign of wear on Luca himself. The man had apparently slept like a baby through the attack and was ready to take on the world. A good thing, too. A healer was what this town most desperately needed now.

"Hmm, hundred or so witnesses, aside from the subjects … plenty of those, though. This will do, this will do," he muttered cheerfully to himself, then winked at Valeria. "Observe! Oh, and if I'm accused of dark magics, I trust you'll defend my good name, all things considered. I couldn't risk it before, but the church can't touch me now."

"Wha—" Valeria started, but Luca's voice was already booming over the square: "I am Luca of Newhaven, master of the arcane arts! Remember that name well, for today you shall witness a miracle like no other!"

Luca threw his arms up into the air, and it was as if lighting struck him from the clear sky. Valeria averted her eyes and could see some of the crowd covering theirs as well. The burst of power was visible even to the layman.

Valeria forced her gaze back and analyzed the vortex of energy that obscured Luca from sight. It was composed of hundreds, maybe thousands of strands of magical force streaking up into the sky. The streams separated in midair and rained back down, striking all the people around them—the sick, the injured and the dead alike. One strand even struck her, and she felt her weariness subside, like she'd slept particularly well last night.

As the vortex dissipated, Luca's triumphant form became visible once again. Then he fell limp onto the ground, a beatific smile frozen upon his lips.

"You bastard ..." Valeria uttered under her breath.

The sick who had been waiting for healing were crying tears of happiness, their ailments gone.

The wounded who had been limping toward the square were running now, overjoyed at the miracle.

The piles of corpses were waking up, dazed and confused, but none the worse for wear.

"You bastard!" Valeria shouted at her master's corpse. "This is useless to me! This is useless to anyone!" Then she caught herself and glanced around. Everybody was too excited by their dead friends coming back to life to have noticed her indiscretion.

Valeria gritted her teeth. It all made perfect sense now. Luca had traded his life for what truly was a fair exchange to him: a whole townful of people. No doubt he'd paid for curing deadly ailments with minor aches or somesuch, because that's what other people's lives were worth to him. All for his personal glorification.

But Valeria could never be so callous, and thus never work half the good that Luca had.

Unless ...

Unless, perhaps, she were to find someone who yearned to be better than they were. Kind, compassionate, modest.

She could make herself worse in exchange; colder and more hungry for recognition.

Then she, too, could work miracles.

REKINDLED

NERA KNEW SOMETHING WAS AMISS as soon as she noticed the crow cawing on her porch a mere three weeks after the fall equinox. Mother's next letter, no doubt wishing Nera well in all her endeavors, wasn't due until the winter solstice.

The crow cawed and pushed a small container tied to his leg toward Nera.

"Just a moment, Wisp. I'll get you your treat," she said to the crow. Intelligent as the familiar was, he was still a crow. Headstrong, willful, proud—just as Mother liked it. He would run errands for her, to be sure, but he expected to be properly compensated for his time and effort.

Wisp bobbed his head up and down in acknowledgment. Nera entered her single-room hut, suitable for an independent medicine woman in her late twenties. A simple stone fireplace in the corner to keep her warm, a bed to let her rest her bones, and a stool and a table to write on. A shelf to the left of the fireplace held jars of herbs and tinctures of various kinds, and the shelf to the right was reserved for more mundane foodstuffs.

She reached into a jar on the latter shelf, pulled out a handful of nuts, and returned outside.

She crouched next to Wisp, placed the nuts on the porch, and said: "Here you go. Could I have Mother's letter now, please?"

The crow tilted his head, a gesture that Nera had learned to take for a smile and proceeded to tinker with the string on his leg. As soon as he'd gotten the container free, he picked it up and placed it in Nera's hand. Then he turned to regard the pile of nuts.

"Could you wait a while so I can see if an immediate reply is called for?"

Wisp picked up a nut in his beak, bobbed his head up and down, and proceeded to bite into the treat.

"Thanks," Nera said with a smile. "I'll try to make it quick." Then she went inside and opened the window next to the table. The sun was still high, and the southwestern view was good for evening reading.

Nera popped the container's cap, dug out a small scroll, and spread it onto the table. Despite her age, Mother's hand was as steady as ever. Nera had to squint to make out the tiny letters:

Dear Nera,

I hope this letter finds you well. It occurs to me that we've barely spoken anything of import for the better part of the decade. I'd like for us to get to know each other again, and give Wisp some proper exercise. What say you?

Regards,
Raziela

Nera chuckled. This was a change from the formal pleasantries they usually exchanged four times a year. Not an unwelcome one, though. They'd just sort of drifted apart since Mayview had lost its previous medicine woman and Nera had answered the call. But maybe it was time to reconnect.

Dipping her pen in the inkwell, Nera wrote her agreement on the blank side of the scroll, then rolled the message back into the cylinder. Wisp jumped up on the table, having eaten his fill, and Nera tied the message to his leg. "Thanks, Wisp. Give Mother my best," she said.

Wisp cawed and took off through the open window, disappearing into the sun.

•   •   •

Two days later the crow returned, and twice a week hence. The pace was such that it was all Nera could do to think of something to write back before Wisp would be knocking on her door again.

Mother shared her memories of the early years, how she'd juggled raising a baby and serving her community, not always to her own satisfaction. She wrote about how she'd kept Nera busy with learning about healing herbs and tinctures as soon as she was out of the crib. She recounted how distraught she'd been when the whooping cough had spread throughout the village, Nera falling ill among the rest, but how her medicinal arts had managed to triumph over it in the end.

And she wrote of the bittersweet sensation of Nera coming into her own and leaving for Mayview, of her regret over letting their contact largely lapse while busying herself in her own responsibilities. Nera sent a reply reminding her that they'd both had their hand in that.

As the year marched on and the winter solstice approached, Mother suggested that Nera join her for a quiet celebration. Nera happily agreed and prepared for the journey.

•   •   •

Nera's old home was as it had ever been. The stone house was twice the size of Nera's own, and had twice the rooms—gratitude of a village well served. A diverse herb garden dominated the front yard, its lushness only slightly reined in by the mild winter air. The rest of the surroundings were as nature wished.

A caw from above welcomed her as she approached the front door by way of the narrow garden path. Nera looked up and saw Wisp circling in the sky. She gave him a little wave, and the crow dove down and in through a cracked window at the front.

"Ah, she's here?" asked a familiar voice from her childhood. There was an affirmative caw. "Come on in!" Mother hollered. "It's not as if I've put a bolt on the door!"

Nera chuckled. "Didn't expect you had!" The hinges creaked with age as she opened the door to the main room. It hadn't changed a bit since Nera last laid eyes on it, except for the large piles of paper in every corner of the room. The walls were otherwise lined with shelves full of one odd thing or another. To the left of the door stood a table with some dishes and cutlery on it. A tattered couch lay near the fireplace.

The door to her mother's room was open, not that there was any chance of closing it without clearing some of the clutter first. Nera peeked in, barely catching sight of Wisp's tail at the window as he took off into the air again. Mother sat at her desk with a pile of empty papers on her left and full ones on her right, her quill furiously working on the half-filled sheet in front of her.

Mother raised her smiling face toward Nera, but her hand continued scribbling as she spoke: "Welcome, welcome, my child. It's good to see you after so long."

"Too long, Mother. It's good to see you, and that you're as vital as ever. It's not just my correspondence keeping your hand busy, then?" Nera asked, trying to insert some levity into the obvious question.

Mother's smile widened. "No, it's not. But it is one of my more pleasant pastimes."

"What're you working on now?" Nera asked.

"Come and have a look, why don't you?"

Nera came closer and tilted her head to get a better view of her mother's writing:

Nera came closer and tilted her head to get a better view of my writing, said the latest line of text as soon as her mother had finished with it. Nera raised her eyebrow. *Nera raised her eyebrow*, Mother added.

Nera sat on the spare stool next to the desk. "Well, at least from what I can tell, you're writing what I'm doing *after* the fact," she said matter-of-factly.

Her mother chuckled. "Right you are, my girl. You always were quick to notice such things." Her hand continued to write. A quick glance told Nera that yes, her mother was writing her own words down as well.

"For what purpose are you narrating everything we do, if you don't mind me asking?"

"Why, what does one usually make notes for? I want to be able to remember my dear daughter's visit. Ah. 'Nera pursed her lips, perhaps thinking my memory isn't what it used to be.' My recollection is fine, dear. It's just, you know, sometimes writing things down helps in forming memories. Ones that last."

"I see." What with the piles of text in the house, Nera wondered if her mother's scribal habits had gotten a bit out of control. Then again, Mother seemed very present even as her hand wrote down the minutiae of their encounter. Perhaps she should reserve judgment. "Well, if you think my visit is worth jotting down, who am I to argue?" She gave her mother a smile.

"Worth it indeed. Now, if you wouldn't mind lending a hand, we should probably be getting ready for supper, and I've had my hands full in writing my memoirs. I do have some sweets stashed for the solstice, so fear not, it'll be more than potatoes."

Nera laughed, and they proceeded to the main room to prepare supper, Mother taking her quill and some sheets along.

•　　　•　　　•

As they dug into their vegetable casserole at the table, Mother noted that she'd want to know all about Nera's life in Mayview, everything Nera hadn't had time to go through yet in their correspondence.

Mother dipped her quill in ink and made notes as Nera recounted some of her older trials and triumphs from back when she'd just started out on her own. Easing births, setting bones, pulling teeth. More often than not, she'd managed to eke out a victory for life, and from the occasional defeat she'd made a point to learn what went wrong, to better be prepared for the next challenge.

Given a less-than-subtle prod from her mother, Nera mused that there was, indeed, a man in the village who'd been casting eyes at her. However, she was doing just fine on her own, and she'd kept away from such attentions thus far as she wasn't certain that was quite her thing. Mother laughed at that, telling the blushing Nera that she didn't have to have any one thing if she didn't so choose, or, indeed, any thing at all.

The two talked well into the night, taking a break only to go outside and see the midnight stars as they were on the darkest night of the year. Eventually the late hour got the better of them, and they fell asleep together in Mother's bed.

The next day it was time for Nera to leave, as it was not good for a medicine woman to stay away from her village for too long. The two exchanged hearty goodbyes and promised to continue keeping Wisp busy.

Nera left for home, her step heavy only for the voluminous pages of medicinal lore her mother had bestowed on her, fresh out of the quill.

•　　•　　•

Three weeks after her visit, Nera woke up to a loud cawing from the door. Everything was dark, and Nera felt that she hadn't had a proper night's sleep. Wisp must've flown to her across the night. That was unusual, to say the least.

She rose to sit and fumbled for the lantern and tinderbox by her bedside. Getting a flame going was a moment's work. Then she dragged her feet to the door and opened it.

Wisp was standing on the porch, his head low, with a cylinder that must've been ten inches long beside him. There was no string, though the cylinder had a couple of clawholds.

"Oh, my. You've been brave," Nera said.

Wisp ruffled his feathers and stepped inside wearily, leaving the cylinder out on the porch.

"I'll take care of that for you," Nera said, picking up the package and closing the door. "You must be starving. Let me get you a little something before I open this."

Wisp cawed approvingly as Nera set some nuts and dried berries on a plate in front of him. Then she sat on her desk and opened the cylinder in the light of the lantern.

Out popped a single scroll along with a black quill pen, similar to what her mother had used when Nera was visiting. She examined the quill in her hand. The feather had perfect vanes with a smooth shine to them. The tip was sharp, suitable for precision work. Such quills were often from crows.

"This yours?" Nera asked Wisp.

The familiar cawed and bobbed his head up and down.

"From a molting, I trust?" she continued. That was, after all, the usual way.

Wisp nodded again, then turned back to his nuts.

Nera flashed a brief smile. "A considerate gift, to be sure, but you wouldn't have had to fly all night to bring it," she said as she laid the pen down on the table and spread out the scroll.

Dear Nera,

I thank you for a truly blessed time these past few months. Our correspondence has been a wonderful way for me to reminisce, to take stock of my life through writing. I must confess I had an ulterior motive for this, but do not doubt my sincerity in everything I've written, for it was a necessity in fulfilling my other purpose as well. I'm proud of you, and though I taught you to be a medicine woman, I fear I may have concentrated on that overmuch, leaving you to teach yourself to be a proper human being. It is of some consolation that you've done a good job of it.

I have lived a good, long life, and I could feel it in my bones that this would be my last winter. So I poured out my soul through this here quill, to keep it when my body was done.

That time has come. Please take care of Wisp for me, and arrange a proper burial for my earthly remains. All of my wisdom, such as it is, is yours to find in my writings at home.

Or you may find it in your hand, as I am here for you, if you'll have me.
Love,

The letter ended without a signature.

After staring at the scroll for a few moments, Nera became aware of movement in her peripheral vision and turned to look. The quill was hovering over the inkwell in a quiet gesture of request, rotating as if suspended from above by a thread. Nera's mouth fell open.

Moving as if in a dream, she opened the inkwell. The pen carefully dipped in, swooped up to the letter and signed it: *Raziela.* Mother's handwriting, no doubt about it.

Wisp hopped onto the table and nuzzled Nera. She pushed back softly, her eyes still on the hovering quill. Wisp hopped over her arm and nuzzled the quill, which caressed his feathers gently. Wisp tilted his head contentedly.

A single tear rolled down Nera's cheek.

"Welcome home, Mom."

PICKING TIME

Y OU'VE SEARCHED FOR your little sister for quite a while already when Mom shouts your names from the door.

"Just a moment," you yell back. "I haven't found Willow yet."

"All right, but be quick about it," Mom agrees, and goes back inside.

It shouldn't take long. You've already checked Willow's usual hiding spots: the hole beneath the house, behind the tree in the yard, and all the bushes. You've even ran around the house, and it didn't sound like Willow was cheating by running ahead of you.

You go check the rainwater barrel, but even that is empty. You scratch your head while looking around, when a suppressed laugh from the forest grabs your attention. A gray tunic flashes behind a tree, well outside your yard.

"Willow! I see you! Behind the tree by the path! Come here now!"

Willow's grinning face appears above the hem of the tunic. "That took a while!" she says and approaches the yard.

"You're not supposed to go that far!" you protest.

"There's no rule against it," Willow says matter-of-factly.

You frown. It's true, though. Willow just hasn't wanted to wander outside the yard alone. She tends to be a bit anxious even when going together with you, though she doesn't complain.

"Ah, Willow. Good, you're found," Mom says from the door. You turn around to look. She has wooden buckets for you two. "Go and pick us some bilberries. They should be in season. Remember our spot?"

You nod eagerly. "Yes, Mom." While you can find some where ever you go, there was a special spot teeming with them within walking distance. For filling entire buckets without using up your whole day, you'd best go there before anyone else beat you to it.

"Stay on this side of the cliffs, then," Mom reminds you , as always when you're going into the woods.

"Yes, yes," you say, grab the buckets and start skipping along the forest path. While the buckets are still empty, it's easier to carry them both yourself. It's more balanced, and you don't have to wait for Willow as much. She follows in your footsteps quick enough.

When you make your way to the bilberry spot, you look around the woods in confusion. The undergrowth, usually blue with berries, is almost devoid of bounty.

Willow frowns. "Somebody got here first. Let's go back home?"

You grind your teeth. "Yes they did. But let's look a bit further. We're not yet too far from home."

"Okay," Willow says. You expected some protests, but maybe she really is getting braver. Or Mom's bilberry pie is on her mind.

You split up a bit to cover more area, but you take care not to leave Willow out of your sight. For a while you see only plants picked bare, if even those, but just as you're about to give up, you notice some blue a bit to the right of you. "Here!" you yelp at Willow.

She runs to you, her smile radiant. As you lift your gaze up from the ground, you notice that you've wondered near the cliffs. You mustn't go farther, but this is still fine.

The land is generous with its blue bounty, and the bucket fills up quickly. You feel good about being able to bring food to the family table. You'll probably get some pie for your trouble. Not that you particularly like bilberries—Mom says that's why you're such a trustworthy berry picker—but the crust is always good, and Mom takes care to put fewer berries in one corner of the pie.

"There's more over there," Willow says, pointing toward the narrow cliff pass nearby. Her bucket is only half full. The telltale blue around her lips betrays the why of it. She likes the berries a little too well for the job.

"Fine, but don't go into the pass," you remind your little sister. "Pick whatever's on this side. Then we'll head home."

"Good," she says and skips toward the berries.

You turn back to your patch, and soon top off your bucket.

"Willow, I'm done here. How're you?" you ask, but there's no reply. You glance around the forest, taking a few side steps to look behind the nearby trees, but she's nowhere to be seen.

"Willow!" you shout. "Not funny!"

Nothing.

The forest's not too thick. If she was on this side of the cliffs, you'd see her. There's but one place to look. You leave your bucket of berries and run into the pass.

The shadows of the cliffs surround you. The chill penetrates deep into your bones quicker than you'd expect. You keep shouting for Willow, but only the echo responds.

Soon the cliffs open into another patch of the forest, lush and full of bounty, glistening in the evening dew. The variety of berries is astonishing. You didn't even know raspberries grew around here, or that they'd be in season.

You're not here for the berries, though. "Willow!" you shout again, to no avail. Studying the undergrowth, you find a faint path through freshly trodden plants. You quickly grab a handful of raspberries to help keep your nerves in check and rush onward.

The forest canopy is thick, yet somehow the shadows are light and the way forward clear. One by one the raspberries disappear into your mouth as you run. Just as you swallow the final berry, you lose track of the path. You try to stop to find it again, but your legs keep moving of their own accord, taking you deeper and deeper into the woods.

Your heart skips a beat, but for Willow, you try to keep your head cool. You wave your arms around a bit, just to make sure they still work. The right one doesn't. As you stare at it in horror, you see a glint in the air above it. Squinting, you can make out a few water droplets forming a straight line that reaches upward from your hand. Now that you know what you're looking for, a quick glance finds similar traces of strings attached to your feet.

You've seen marionettes on the market. You know what the strings are for.

There's no time to lose. It's all over if they catch your remaining hand. Quick as lightning, you make a wide sweeping motion with the arm and stumble onto the ground as your legs become yours again.

A bright laughter echoes from the canopy. You raise your head from the bushes and gasp. A few steps in front of you stands a Fae creature. He's your size, but you know better than to think him a child. Every part of him is green, his skin as pale as his hair is dark. He has no clothes, though the long hair contorts to cover his modesty. His head is slightly tilted as he regards you with his vacant eyes. There is a delighted smile on his lips. It reminds you of your sister's smile when she found out the secret of the matryoshka doll: a toy that has more to it than seems at first.

You've heard all the stories about dealing with the Fae. It always, always ends badly. You have to get out of here, get help. Maybe Mom and Dad know someone. Someone who can come in and find your sister for you. You push yourself up, ready to spring back toward the pass, hoping that you might be able to outrun the fairy now that you know to watch out for the strings.

As you get to your feet, you gasp in shock as you see not one, but two Willows lying unconscious on the ground. You can't run now. Who knows what would happen to your sister then?

You stand frozen for a moment. The fairy tilts his head the other way, the eerie smile still on his face.

The stories suggest you should be assertive but polite. You clear your throat. "M-mister Fae, I think you have found something of mine. If I can have her back, we'll be on our way and not bother you again."

The smile has teeth now. "As you admit, find it I did, and here what you find, you keep. But I like you, so I propose a game."

A shiver runs down your spine. This is exactly what every story has warned you about. "What kind of a game?"

"You've caught me in a generous mood, you have. Your sister is here. Pick the one you'd like to take with you, and I will let you both go free. This I swear by my name." As the fairy speaks, you notice the sharpness of the teeth behind the smile.

The Fae may deceive, but they don't lie, and far be it from them to smear their names. You'll just have to figure out which Willow is real, and which is a changeling, or what have you.

You study the girls carefully, finding no difference. Even the bilberry spots on the lips and the birthmarks behind the ear match. But then, as you squint, you notice a few droplets of dew in the air. Marionette strings connect one of the Willows to the fairy. He must be using them to keep your real sister still.

You point at the Willow with the strings coming out of her. "I choose this one," you say in a trembling voice.

"A promise made is a promise kept," says the fairy. "Take her, run along, and don't look back. I can't make any promises on behalf of my cousin here." His smile is downright feral now.

You strike at the strings, pull your groggy sister up and start dragging her toward the pass. Now in control of herself, she soon gets her bearings and starts running with you. There is a thud behind you, but you take the fairy's advice to heart. You just run, never looking back.

•   •   •

The new bilberry season has roused memories of last year, try as you might to keep them buried. You glance at Willow, who's sitting by the window. She's staring into the forest, her eyes vacant. She does that sometimes—but then, doesn't everyone?

Her head turns toward you. As her gaze meets yours, the shine is suddenly back in her eyes, as if she'd just forgotten to wear it for a moment. There's no part of her that doesn't seem like your sister now.

You can't help but wonder if you can ever know for sure if you got the right one out. You've made note of some changes in her habits. She seems more at home in the forest, now, and she likes to fiddle with her long hair in front of her. But then, isn't change a part of growing up?

Would even she herself know it if she was a changeling? She says she doesn't remember anything of the ordeal a year ago. Maybe it was the shock, or maybe the Fae messed with her memories. You've never tried to fill in the gaps for her. You'd much rather you didn't remember any of it either, after all.

Mom's touch on your shoulder rouses you from your thoughts. She hands you a plate.

It's bilberry pie, your favorite.

THE SOULBANE

THE LAST THREE DRAGON RIDERS sat solemnly around the crackling campfire. For twelve generations, their people had roamed the world on the backs of their dragons, never stopping for long, always looking over their shoulders.

Except, perhaps, once every few generations or so, when they'd forget why they were the Dragon Riders. They'd find a place relatively unscathed by the spreading droughts and settle down to pursue a more peaceful life. The elders' warnings about staying still would be dismissed as ramblings.

This had happened three times, and thrice the White Knight had come for them, butchering everyone he could with his Soulbane. The survivors had fled into the ever-spreading deserts.

Loren gnawed on the group's last strip of dried meat. Her noble lineage didn't count for anything these days, but being with child still had its privileges. She was vaguely aware that in some other world she'd have been a princess, perhaps a queen, though it wasn't something she'd bring up with the others. They were all in the same boat now.

When Loren had swallowed her last mouthful, she sighed and brushed some wayward strands of hair off her face. "This is it. Rhys has given us his last."

"Peace upon him," Jona said quietly from behind his large hands. Rhys had been his mount, his companion. The bond between rider and dragon was sacred, but that hadn't stopped Jona from partaking in the meat, even if reluctantly. It was of some small comfort that this was what Rhys would've wanted, or so Jona had told the others. It was probably true. Dragons were noble creatures, and practical in matters of survival.

"What are we now?" Karin muttered under her breath, dark eyes staring intently into the dark, dead forest. She was the last of the lore keepers, and carried the history of her people in her mind—or as much of it as her mother had had time to teach her before she'd passed. "What are we, that we've eaten the last of what made us who we are?"

"We're alive, that's what we are," Loren said and took a careful sip from her waterskin.

"For today. What of tomorrow?" Karin insisted.

"You live one day at a time. That is also what it means to be a Dragon Rider," Loren said, caressing her belly. Maternal instincts still resisted succumbing to the reality of their situation.

Jona scoffed. "What's the use of living when the whole world's crumbling to dust? May the White Knight take us all."

The others startled at that, but only for a moment. It was easy enough to shrug off old wives' tales when you had more immediate problems.

"It's just the three of us. Even if he was real, we'd probably have to be the last people alive for him to bother," Karin said.

"You are," said a tired voice from the shadows beyond the campfire.

Panic-stricken, the Riders sprang up, drew their blades, and faced the direction of the voice. A soft white glow in the shape of a sword slowly faded into existence. The weapon was held by a pale man dressed in tattered rags that might have once been white. His expression was otherwise blank, but there was a glimmer of hope in his eyes, a fervent wish fulfilled.

Loren gasped, her eyes on the sword. "The Soulbane!" Reflexively she protected her belly with her off hand.

"I could tell you this was for your own good, but it's proven to be as futile as any fight you try to put up," the White Knight said, casually advancing on Jona's massive figure. "I'm empowered by the souls of millions. You will join them, and my task will finally be complete."

Karin sensed an opening and charged the knight from his side, her blade slashing through the air fast as lightning—but there was a blur in the air, and then the glowing sword protruded out of her back. She let out a blood-chilling scream as her skin tightened. The sword pulsed brighter, and her body fell to the ground as dust.

"One down, three to go," the Knight mused.

Loren panicked. "Jona, please! He can sense the baby! He can't have the baby!"

Jona hesitated for but a moment before plunging his sword into Loren's stomach. She fell on her knees, then down on the ground. A look of desperation appeared in the White Knight's eyes. In a flash, he was there and pierced Loren precisely where Jona had already struck her. Loren's body convulsed, tightened and turned to dust.

A tiny figure, no larger than a fist, remained behind. "Damn. Damn! Thrice damned! Was I too late?" the Knight cursed, casually smacking Jona aside. Then he took his sword and slashed the tiny head of the fetus with its blade.

The sword pulsed again, and he let out a relieved sigh. "I just missed. Forgot it could happen. One soul masks another."

Jona scrambled back to his feet. His sword lay at the Knight's feet. He glanced around for other weapons within reach and found none.

"Why? What have we done that you've chased us down for generations? Isn't it enough that the land itself tries to kill us? Or is it just that? You're feeding off of us because there's nothing else to feed on?"

The Knight raised his chin up and let out a laugh, and his laughter was the most pure, vibrant and joyful thing that Jona had ever heard.

"It's not the land that works against us, it's the Sun. This world can no longer support life as we know it." The Knight walked slowly toward Jona, brandishing his weapon. "Swords, however, need no food, no water, no air. Powered by millions upon millions of souls dancing as one, melding together, creating souls anew, magic can outlast suns. All that is needed is for someone to bear the screams of those souls as they move on." The Knight's eyes were hard and determined, yet full of tears.

"I ... I don't understand," Jona said.

"You will," the White Knight promised and plunged his sword into Jona's chest. He heard the man's scream and watched as he turned to light and dust.

Then the Knight spread out his arms and turned around full circle, listening to the quiet song of the sword in his mind. No souls anywhere in any of the four winds.

Except one.

"Far away from those four," he said perhaps to himself, perhaps to the sword. After years of solitude he wasn't quite sure anymore. "So that I might still blend in."

Then he raised his sword for one final time.

●　　　●　　　●

The Knight materialized in a lush meadow, next to a small pond full of crystal clear water. A group of three children were splashing at each other, altogether too engrossed in their play to notice him.

Perhaps it was better that way, as the knight's rags had disappeared. His bare body was young, clean, and healthy. He marveled at his right hand, empty and unburdened. The sword he had forged so long ago, and carried across centuries, was gone as well. Or had it been the sword that had carried him, kept him going for as long as it took to finish his task?

"Oy!" said a voice behind him. "Haven't seen anyone appear like that in ages."

Turning around, the knight came face to face with man dressed in a simple but comfortable looking blue tunic. He was apparently in his prime, but aside from the children, who wasn't? That was how he'd made this world, a refuge from time and want.

For the first time in centuries, a smile spread across the knight's face. "I have a feeling I'll be among the last. Show me around, would you?"

ABOUT THE AUTHOR

Mikko Rauhala is a bilingual Finnish science fiction author. He often writes his stories in both languages, which can get frustrating when there's no one else to blame for the occasional dual meanings.

Informed by his master's degree in intelligent systems, he's most at home in hard science fiction settings, though he's not exclusive and likes to cross genres. Whether the subject is steam powered gnomes or universal quantum suicide, Rauhala enjoys taking an eccentric premise and bringing it to its logical conclusion. As befits a Finn, his plot-driven narrative is often seasoned with a touch of dark, dry humor.

Rauhala's Finnish short fiction has been published in collections and other media, and he has a national Atorox award nomination to show for it. His English credits include coauthoring *Infinite Metropolis* (Aurelia Leo, 2020) and "Rekindled" in *Best Vegan SFF of 2020* (Metaphorosis, 2021).

ALSO BY THE AUTHOR

THE PAPERCLIP WAR

Mikko Rauhala

After a nebulous Enemy destroys Earth, the remnants of humanity settle on Mars. Not only does this civilization survive, but they thrive, creating advancements for the rest of the solar system.

Available from Water Dragon Publishing in
hardcover, trade paperback, and digital editions
waterdragonpublishing.com

YOU MIGHT ALSO ENJOY

STRAINED SIGMA BONDS

Arasibo Campeche

Embark on adventures to discover stories about science, magic, the tarot, Haitian vodou, the clash of epistemologies, and addiction.

SOMETIMES AFTER DARK

J Dark

Explore the past, future, and triumphs of the human soul.

CORPORATE CATHARSIS
THE WORK FROM HOME EDITION

The pandemic came and the world changed. Lives have changed; work has changed. The boundaries between reality and fantasy have become as blurred as those between life and work.

THE FUTURE'S SO BRIGHT

Out of the darkness of the present comes the light of the days ahead …

Available from Water Dragon Publishing in
hardcover, trade paperback, and digital editions
waterdragonpublishing.com